I0654906

Confessions Of A Convenience Store Clerk

Richard Henshaw

Copyright © 2014 by Richard Vargon.
All rights reserved.

ISBN 13: 978-0-692-26676-2

Without limiting the rights under copyright reserved above, no
part of this publication may be reproduced, stored in or introduced into a retrieval system, or transmitted, in any form, or by
any means (electronic, mechanical, photocopying, recording,
or
otherwise), without the prior written permission of the copyright holder.

The scanning, uploading, and distribution of this book via the
Internet or via any other means without the permission of the
copyright holder is illegal and punishable by law. Please pur-
chase only authorized electronic editions, and do not partici-
pate in or encourage electronic piracy of copyrighted materials.
Your support of the author's rights is greatly appreciated.

This is a work of fiction. Names, characters, businesses,
places, events, and incidents are either the products of the
author's
imagination or used in a fictitious manner. Any resemblance
to actual persons, living or dead, or actual events is purely
coincidental.

"The best way to get over a woman
is to turn her into literature."

Henry Miller

1

It's 2:00 in the afternoon, and I'm sitting here in my dark-ened living room, in my little hot box of an apartment. It's April 1ˢᵗ, but we're already in the middle of a heat wave that feels like August. I'm watching it pour down rain through one of the only two windows that provide what little breeze the day has to offer.

I don't have air conditioning and I'm too cheap to buy a fan. There is a ceiling fan in the bedroom. It doesn't do much. I'm afraid to use it at night, anyway because I have a fear of it falling from the ceiling, and cutting me to ribbons. How would that look on the evening news?

"Tonight investigators for the Allegheny County Sheriff's Department have confirmed that a man was found naked and sliced to pieces in his low rise borough apartment. Apparently, a ceiling fan somehow worked its way loose and performed the grisly act, as it fell onto the victim, who was asleep in bed. Authorities refuse to describe the scene, but a forensics team member, who wishes to remain anonymous, has told us that the man's penis was found in a shoe in one corner of the room.

"Though investigators have ruled it an accident, we here at Channel 11 News are of the strong opinion that due to the extreme extent that the fan went to dismember its victim in this way that this was an act that was performed by a fan that knew its victim and therefore should be considered foul play."

Well, thank you Channel 11 News for telling the world that I sleep in the nude! And hey, I know the fan is not gonna fall on me. Though anything is possible in my mind. I probably only think that, because my neighbor Otis had claimed that his had fallen on him. To be fair, you must consider that Otis is a drunk.

I call him Otis, but his real name is Gary. He's in bad shape, and about to be evicted. I knocked on his door the other day, because I wanted to warn him. I could hear him moaning something mournful.

I said, "Gary, it's me, I gotta tell ya something."

"Gary's not here man," he groaned.

I said, "Gary, it's important... Open up."

"Gary's not here, man... Go away."

I was beginning to believe that I had somehow slipped into a parallel universe. I tried the knob, and slowly pushed on the door, half afraid of what I would see. What I saw was Otis sitting on his couch, arms and hands stretched out, as if warming himself by a fire. In front of him, on the coffee table, sat a propane heater connected to a propane tank. It was 90 degrees outside. It had to be 110 degrees in his living room.

I said, "Gary what the fuck are you doing?"

He says, "What the fuck does it look like I'm doin'? In case you haven't noticed, it's freezing in here. The fuckers turned off my electricity, and I got no heat."

I felt really bad when I called the landlord, and told him what Otis was up to. Hell, I didn't want him to burn the place down. It's a huge wooden house, over a hundred years old, with eight tiny apartments crammed into it. It wouldn't take much. The next morning, Otis was given his last warning. He's been warned a lot.

I guess the other tenants can't deal with Otis' ranting and raving in front of the building, about how unchristian-like the landlord is, and how evil the rest of us are. I don't think Beverly, the girl who lives in apartment 6, was thrilled when he tried to pee out the flames of hell that were nipping at her screen door, as she sat breast-feeding her kid on the living room couch.

. . . . .

I'm sitting here procrastinating because I just read a letter from my ex-wife. She won't leave me alone. It's ironic, because the first few months after we split up, I wouldn't leave her alone. I called her, wrote poetry for her, sent her flowers, and showered her with gifts. She told me I should have been doing that while we were married.

I have to admit she was right. While we were married, I was not a very good husband. I was immature and still on the wild side. I was only eighteen. The whole idea of marriage was ridiculous. I wasn't ready to be married. The crazy part was that it was my idea.

Sara Pickens was my girlfriend in high school. I think she only chose me, because my best friend Dane was already taken by a girl named Shannon Morrison. Sara played nice with Shannon, but deep down, she despised her.

Sara and I didn't have much in common. Even back then she already had a life plan. In the yearbook she wrote, *See you at the country club.* I was lucky if I could see into the next day. I never understood that high society talk. She was just a country girl. But it was one of the things I admired about her.

Anyway, what we did have in common was sex. Sara is gorgeous, and she has the hottest pussy I've ever had the pleasure to bury my face into. She knows how to fuck. Some girls expect you to make them come, but not Sara. She used me like a human dildo. She knows how to make her pussy work for her. She could come three times by the time I did, and trust me, I'm no master of restraint.

I couldn't resist her charms and she has plenty of 'em. You know how it is when you first fall for someone. All you do is fuck. Tables, kitchen counters, the trusty woods, any surface that could hold our weight. Once, as I sat on the toilet about to loosen my load, she came into the room, sat on my lap and screwed me right on the throne. I had to tighten that thing back down to the floor afterwards.

I'll never forget the time we were helping Dane and Shannon move into their place and we snuck into an empty bedroom. Sara bent over and propped her hands against the wall like she was waiting to be frisked by the cops. When I pulled her shorts aside to enter her, she was already so wet and turned on that she almost came before I was completely inside of her.

Most girls would be nervous to do something like that, but not Sara. The prospect of getting caught turned her on even more. She thought it was hilarious that while our unsuspecting homemakers were unpacking in the next room, we had already christened their new home before they could, and especially before Shannon could.

I think they knew something was up though, because when we came out of the room they looked at us kind of funny. What we thought was funny was that we were both wearing sunglasses when we did it, and our poker faces never gave us away. Although Sara wouldn't let me forget that for most of the rest of the day, she'd had to live with wet panties.

Sara had no fear of getting pregnant. She had fallen from a ladder, while helping her mother paint their living room ceiling. She'd had surgery, and her doctor told her she'd never be able to conceive. So we fucked like banshees, and on the night of our senior prom, she conceived.

I'll never forget how good she felt that night, her pussy wrapped around me, tight, as she slid up and down my shaft, still wearing her prom dress, in the back of my Ford Bronco. It was a magic night, and somehow I knew when I came into her, harder than I ever had before, that something had happened.

By then we were crazy for each other. So, when she sat next to me on the couch, and whispered those four little words into my ear, "your boys can swim," I just automatically proposed to her. The scary part was asking her dad's permission. Miraculously, he didn't kill me. He was proud that I was willing to man up, and do the right thing.

I should have known things weren't going to work out when Sara's mother slipped on the steps in front of the church and broke her leg on our wedding day. A couple of weeks later Sara miscarried, and then everything went downhill from there. She never did grieve the child or become despondent. Instead, she became determined to point out every little thing I did wrong, which wasn't a stretch, cause I did lots of things wrong.

It took less than six months for her to dump me. I knew Sara was cold, but on one unusually warm October night, she proved to me just how cold she could be. We had been celebrating Halloween, by smearing melted chocolate bars onto our genitals, and then licking it off. Sara had already come once from the candy play, and by the time that she'd climbed on top of me, she had become as horny as I'd ever seen her.

We were good enough together that I could usually hold on until, she'd climaxed as much as she'd liked, but this night, her lusty spirit had possessed me in ways that I'd never felt before, and I knew that I wasn't going to be able to hang on much longer. Suddenly, she had such an intense orgasm that I'd swear I could feel it come out of her, and ripple down my shaft.

My dick had begun to pulsate and swell, as it usually does when I'm about to blow, but then she rolled off of me, and smiled.

"I got mine," she giggled, and then she slid off of the bed, and left the room.

I didn't know whether to laugh or cry, but I was about to finish myself off, and from the kitchen she yelled, "Don't you dare!"

For some reason, I just laid there wondering what had just happened, and after about fifteen minutes, she came back into the room and climbed back on top of me.

She fucked me, until she came again, and then she said, "Now, Joshua."

I wasn't about to wait this time. I began to fill her, before the sound of my name had a chance to clear her throat.

She looked down at me and the expression on her face said it all. I gazed into her eyes, and watched as they welled up with sadness, until a single tear rolled down her cheek, and fell to my lips. It was then that I could see all of the pain that she'd been carrying inside of her all those months. But I guess it only took that one tear to shed that pain, because in another second, it was gone.

Within that second, I watched an expression of pure hatred form around her eyes and mouth, so clear that when she said, "I want a divorce," I already knew she was gonna say it.

Then she turned her gaze toward the bedroom door and said, "Trick or fuckin' treat, motherfucker."

She patted my chest and went into the bathroom to take a shower.

. . . . .

I fought to keep her, but it was fruitless. She had already found someone else. I knew she still cared about me, because until they consummated their marriage she continued having sex with me. She cared about me, but I don't think she liked me. She blamed me for everything. I accepted it. I think she slept with me because she felt sorry for me, and because a woman's got to have it, too. She needed a lot of it.

When she stopped giving it to me, I protested. I was hurt. I had begun to believe we might get back together. She made it clear that wasn't going to happen.

I once made the mistake of telling her that I loved her as I was about to come, and she stopped in mid-stroke and told me, "If you ever say that again while we're having sex, I'll cut you off."

About a week later, I said it, again. She cut me off.

So I started writing her letters hoping that I could somehow convert her back to me. At first, they were romantic. I wrote poems for her, a few she even liked. But it was futile, and as time went on, the letters became accusatory and guilt laden.

She became angry and hurtful towards me. I never realized that all those letters were doing was making her feel bad. Eventually, I got it and stopped.

A few months later Sara and her husband moved to Arizona. It's funny because after a while, she started sending me letters. She wasn't mad at me anymore and mostly wanted to know what was going on. I wrote back a couple of times, but then I stopped. She didn't and it's been a while, like two years worth of while. She's starting to get pissed. She says if I don't write, she'll be mad at me, again. I don't want her to be mad at me, again.

She wants details. She wants dirt. She likes dirt. She wants to know about Shannon Morrison. She wants to know if I've fucked her yet, and soiled her for Dane. I've got plenty of dirt to give her, but I'm still procrastinating. Not because I don't know what to write, but because once I start writing, someone's gonna get hurt.

Sara knows most of the players. She's not worried about hurting anyone. Not Dane, and certainly not Shannon. Well, maybe Dane. Besides, she assures me she's not gonna tell. I'll start the letter tomorrow. I've got to get ready for work. I'm procrastinating about that, too.

2

I hate my job. Not because I'm lazy, which I am, but because I don't like having to be obliged to spend seven hours of my life under someone else's control. I can't get behind the concept. One reason is that I fancy myself to be an artist. I'm a fledgling writer and musician, and I'd like to be able to express myself on my own terms, and in my own time and place. I guess if you're doing something you enjoy then it's not so bad. You might even look forward to it. But this job, not so much to like.

A lot of good-looking women do come into the place. I've met a few that way. I've even been fortunate enough to have had sex with a fellow employee, back in the kitchen. Well, I guess the place does offer decent benefits. When you work in a ma and pa run convenience store, it's not very hard to make up some of the rules.

I'm just not cut out for the hospitality business. I'm a friendly person, but I have to take people in doses. Even if I'm at a righteous party, I have to be able to beat it out of there when I'm ready. My point being that I'm not real down with the idea of being stuck in a place for hours, steppin' up and fetchin' for the man.

So you must feel my pain when I tell you that I've been working at Verity's Market, since I was knee high to a horn-dog. Well, it seems that way, but it's actually been, since I was sixteen. At least I've kept the same job, which is good, because I've worked my way up to decent wages and steady daylight hours. It's also convenient, since I now live about a hundred feet away from the place. Believe it or not, I'm late everyday, anyway.

It's named after Verity, the owner Eugene Lansbury's wife. It's still an old time market, with creaky wooden floors, and shelves overflowing with candy, freezers full of ice cream, and magically, almost any item you can find in a Walmart Superstore. It's the kind of place that brings childhood memories back to life. At least, that's what defectors of this little hamlet tell me when they're back in town for a visit. The place has been in the same spot, since the turn of the last century, and has survived two floods. The Lansbury's are only the third owners, calling the place theirs, since 1960. It's also haunted.

It's haunted first of all, by the spirits who wander in from the town watering hole that's located almost right across the street. It's called the 'Sunset Hotel' and it's got a couple of rooms upstairs, and there are one or two charming local ladies that'll take you up there and relieve your tension, one way or another, for a couple of beers and a pack of smokes. It's funny how many "boyfriends" that follow those girls around the store while they pick up a few things for the house. They seem to buy a lot of condoms. I didn't know you can eat condoms.

I also believe that several real ghosts frequent the building. One of them being old Sam McPhee, a farmer that came into the store everyday, since back during the time it was called Mort's Deli. He'd been so used to going there that after his wife died, he just continued hanging out at the place, lending a hand for nothing more than a cup of coffee, and the comfort of feeling wanted. There's a bench outside under the front window that he used to sit on and gab with people for hours on end. His name is engraved on it, and he is still sitting there.

One evening, I was in the back of the store, when I saw a guy walk by, wearing dark blue Dickies work pants, a light blue cotton shirt and suspenders. I didn't think much of it, since I'm used to the regulars having the run of the place. When I looked down the hall, no one was even there. It's a dead end. I would have seen him. Later, when I described the guy to everyone, they almost fell over. I had just described Sam. Those were the clothes he wore every day of his life.

I'm fairly certain that the former owner, Mort Davis has never left the building. Always a stickler for quality, he remains open for business, and means to see to it, that those running the store now, stay on their toes, and give his customers nothing but the best.

Likewise, a former longtime employee named Sally Witherspoon, has hopelessly dedicated herself to covering her shift. She was still working there when I started, and we became close friends. Her husband had died of a heart attack about ten years before, so the store became her home. She fell ill two years ago around Thanksgiving, and never made it back. She follows me all around the place, and I hear her voice all the time.

I'm not a full blown medium, but I am sensitive to some spirit activity. I think I inherited it from my mother. I don't sleep well at night, but when I do, my dreams are always vivid and life-like. In my dreams, I can smell, taste, and feel, and I can remember every detail. I've been told that because of my ability, dreamtime is a good time for spirits to come and tell me their story.

The biggest mystery in life is death. We know plenty of ways to achieve death, but no one can honestly say they're sure what happens, afterwards. People who have faith in religious teachings think they know, but that is what faith is. To believe in someone or something and hope for the best. I don't know what to believe.

. . . . .

The problem with me is that I'm a dreamer. My dream is to make a name for myself, to make my mark in history. Most people live and die, and as time passes, no one ever remembers they existed. They get a stone to mark the spot that their corpse lies in decay, waiting patiently to be consumed by the soil that they came from.

Here lies Joshua Harrison... When he was done, he was done.

I guess someone could steal my identity and go on to become famous for something. But from what I hear I've got bad credit and I'm broke. So, who would want to be me? Or I could cause some type of catastrophe, maybe knock over a lantern while milking my llama, setting my barn ablaze, inadvertently burning the entire city to the ground. I don't know. It all sounds kind of sketchy to me.

At least my mother loves me.

She says, "Who needs to be remembered? When your life is over, God will remember everything you did. Find a nice girl, and have a son to carry on your name. That'll be your mark. That's how your father did it."

Ahh, my father. I never saw much of my dad. I'd never even met him, until I was five years old. Even then he was always in and out. As the story goes, mom and dad had a weekend fling in Frankfurt, Germany where my mother was born. It was during the time my dad was stationed there in the U.S. Army. I guess he fell for her, hard, but she wasn't interested in being in a relationship that lasted more than the time it took to change her underwear.

Apparently, the little surprise my dad had left her wasn't enough to persuade my mom to tell him, at first. So, after his tour of duty was up he went flying off into the sunset on a jet airliner, and by the time he'd reached the promised land, he'd forgotten all about my mother. Eventually, after endless persistence on my part in wanting to know where my father was, my mom got curious.

She found him living in El Paso, Texas with his wife Liz. When dad found out I had come from the fruit of his loins, he was pleased, but unfortunately, at the time, he was about to embark on an expedition to the east coast to investigate claims of unusual goings on at a mountain resort in Roanoke, Virginia.

Evidently, at some point dad had grown bored with his latest arrangement with Liz, and had become heavily interested in the paranormal. His wife did not share his enthusiasm on the subject. Hence, his increasingly frequent departures had begun to leave her lonely and unfulfilled. It didn't help that one of his old lovers Beth Ferguson had joined him on his ghostly adventures.

The excuse my father gave Liz for his sudden desire to chase after things that go bump in the night is what makes it so bizarre.

"He told me that Selena appeared to him one night as a succubus, and had sex with him in our bed, while I slept right next to him," she explained to my mother.

According to legend, Selena Bettencourt was the girlfriend who became unhinged and tried to stab my father to death with a pair of scissors, before turning the weapon on herself, slicing her wrists, and then plunging the shears into her stomach so many times that she had turned her entrails to lasagna. There was blood everywhere, most of it covering my father, as he lay unconscious on the bed.

All of this coming less than a half an hour of taking the life of another girl, who'd been living with them. This attack had been every bit as violent, and even more personal, as Selena's knife had pierced the girl's abdomen several times, and had severed the femoral artery in her leg, in an apparent attempt to mutilate her vagina.

Well, I guess by that point Liz had decided that she'd had it, too. Their relationship had always been on and off through the years, but this time she'd hoped it would last. By the time dad came back from that trip, Liz and my mother had fallen in love.

It seemed fine to me, I was six years old, what did I know? When I heard whimpering coming from their bedroom, I thought my mother was crying. So, when I walked in on them

and saw my mom's head between Liz's legs, I didn't understand it any more than any kid would.

When my father came home, he understood, and then he
went right back out the door. He said he was through with
love. Apparently, this had happened to him before, the whole
girl meets girl thing. After he left that time my mom and Liz
packed up and moved back to Liz's hometown in Pittsburgh,
Pennsylvania. My mother had taught me to speak English, so I
was ready.

3

I've known Dane since we were kids. I love him like a brother. I don't have any brothers or sisters, that I know of. Although, from what I gather, my dad had plenty of opportunities to give me some. So, it's been me and Dane. We did everything together and we still do.

When we were kids, Dane got picked on a lot. He wasn't very big, and he spent a lot of time fighting. The both of us did, actually, cause we always had each other's backs. As Dane grew older, he grew bigger. Now he's like 6' 2" and 220 pounds bigger. Not from lifting weights, but from working on the farm his family lives on.

Now, people don't usually mess with him. He never held a grudge, and he's as even tempered and easy going as a nap under a shade tree on a hot July afternoon. But don't let that fool you. Dane's one of the smartest guys I know. He's very observant of people and not easily fooled.

Dane could have been born in the 1800's. He loves the outdoors and can build a fire without a match. In fact, he refuses to build a fire with a match. He loves to sit around a fire and play music. I do, too, and so do most of our friends.

He can build anything and fix anything. One time, I stopped at his house to borrow a drill. A solenoid on the firewall of my truck was getting wet when it rained and was always crappin' out.

I was gonna move it to another spot, and he said, "Wait a minute."

I thought he was gonna come back with the drill, but instead he had a couple of zip lock sandwich bags and a rubber band. He just wrapped those bags over the solenoid right where it sat, and that thing never gave me trouble, again.

As laid back as Dane is, he can sometimes say things that hurt people's feelings. He won't hesitate to call someone an idiot to their face. He's not being mean, but most people don't realize that. He thinks he's being funny. He only does it to the people that are closest to him. He does it to me. I spend a lot of time trying to explain to our friends, that if Dane picks on you, it means he really likes you.

Dane can be mischievous, too. Like the time he taped the trigger to the handle of the spray head on my mother's kitchen sink, so that when she tried to wet a wash rag to clean up the Dr. Pepper that somehow got spilled all over the table, she got that shower she'd been looking forward to.

The guy has taught me how to do a lot of things. Like shooting a gun and actually hitting the target. He taught me how to ride a motorcycle. He taught me to never ever get stoned while doing either one of them.

Ahh, the music. We both love music. Almost everyone we hang out with plays music. Dane *is* music. It's in his soul. He can play any instrument, and he can sing and harmonize like the high heavens. A lot of the time he records us, always studying how to make the music sound better. For a while I couldn't play. He taught me how to do that, too.

. . . . .

It seems like Dane and Shannon have always been with each other, but they've only really been together since our senior year of high school. Shannon's always been around. I've known her almost as long as I've known Dane. I've always liked her. I've always wanted to be more than friends. Even when we were kids I thought she was beautiful. But Shannon has always had eyes for Dane.

She's a natural beauty. The kind of girl that doesn't need to get all gussied up to look good. Sandy brown hair and a gorgeous body, healthy in all the right places. Pouty, mischievous lips and dark green eyes. She's made out of crème. Feisty as hell if she's comfortable with who you are. Extremely shy around most others.

Shannon had no problem finding the guy she wanted. She just had to wait a while to get him. Dane dated three other girls before he noticed that Shannon had grown up. The first was Nicky Van Houten.

Nicky was one of the mean girls. Totally catty and very hot. The athletic type. She played every sport that they would let a girl compete in. She looked great in a tennis outfit. Captain of the team. Always looking over her shoulder at Dane's younger sister Erin, who was every bit as good a tennis player as she was. Nicky was jealous of Erin, and didn't talk to her until, her interest turned to Dane.

Next thing you know, Erin was in. She did eventually help Nicky get next to Dane. But Erin is a really good person, and she's definitely not a follower. It wasn't long before she came to the conclusion that she wanted no part of Nicky's circle.

Nicky and Dane became one of the popular couples in school, but after a few months she began to act really strange. She had met some people, who turned her on to heroin. She began screwing guys to get money for dope. Dane found out pretty quickly and tried to help her, but when she stole one of his guitars and pawned it, he dumped her. She wound up getting gang raped at a party and had to be hospitalized. A week later someone reported a girl wandering in the woods behind their house, and by the time the cops arrived she'd died of an overdose of pure heroin.

Dane was pretty shook up about it, but a few weeks later, he met someone who was more than willing to help him forget about Nicky. More important, she knew exactly how to make him forget about Nicky. Dane's big old heart needed soothing, but Gabrielle Swanson figured the way to accomplish that task was to first sooth another big old part of his body. And Dane was willing to let her.

Gabrielle lived in a trailer court with her mother, and her twin sister Dawn Marie. Their parents had divorced, and dad was living in Maryland. Dawn Marie was Shannon's best friend. The Swanson sisters are both gorgeous. Both have long curly black hair and look almost identical. It would be hard to tell them apart, except for the fact that Gabrielle is twice as shy as Shannon, and Dawn Marie is a wild woman and very promiscuous.

Dane and Gabrielle only officially dated about a month, simply because neither her sister nor her mother could keep their pants up whenever he was around. When she came home and found her mom screwing Dane on the washing machine, during the spin cycle, she was able to find it in herself to forgive them. But when Dawn Marie got Dane drunk, and pretended to be Gabrielle it was more than she could bear.

The funny part was that Dane knew it was Dawn Marie. He might have had a hard time telling them apart by their looks, but he knew it wasn't Gabrielle's pussy he was eatin'. Evidently Gabrielle's cootch is as bald as a baby's behind. The twin he was fuckin' that particular evening had a fur tree between her legs, and those weren't his own nose hairs he had caught in his teeth.

The bad part was that Shannon told Gabrielle they did it, after Dawn Marie actually bragged to her about it. It effectively ended their friendship, and Gabrielle hated Shannon, too, because she was the one that gave her the news. She knew Shannon wanted Dane and that she didn't seem to mind it at all that she had to betray Dawn Marie to get him.

Then there was Agnes Matheson. A beautiful blonde haired farm girl. She's like a female version of Dane, but make no mistake, she's very female. If she lived in California, she'd be a beach babe. She's just a good girl, and I'm sure she hasn't a mean bone in her body. She's got a hearty laugh and she loves to laugh. Very friendly and thoughtful. Goodhearted and loyal. I'm falling in love with her just thinking about her.

Even though Dane could have lettered in every sport in school, he never got into it. He chose music, instead. He had been in every kind of band the school had to offer, including the marching band, since the eighth grade. By now he had worked his way up to being the band director's right hand guy, and he had complete control of the pit. Dane helped integrate guitars, keyboards, and all sorts of exotic percussion instruments into the show. He built the soundboard and PA system that made it all audible for the audience to enjoy.

Agnes was the captain of the color guard, which by my estimation, is a bunch of very beautiful girls, who wear really awesome outfits, as they dance and swirl through the band formation, twirling flags and streamers. She and Dane actually worked together to choreograph that part of the show with the music. The halftime show had become very sophisticated, and the two of them had spent a lot of time together to help make it happen.

That and the fact they were so good together in every other way, is why I feel really bad about how things went down for her and Dane. Agnes fell very hard for the guy. She loved him more than anything and was totally devoted. She made it clear to him that she would be by his side forever, if he wanted her to. He told her that he did.

That was the only answer she needed to hear the night she gave her virginity to him. Dane told me he loved her. He told me he was gonna propose to her. We were still juniors in high school. I thought they'd be together forever.

By then, I was dating Sara. Even she had to admit that they were a perfect match. So what happened next only made Sara hate Shannon even more. Out of the blue, Dane grew distant towards Agnes, and during spring break, when Agnes went on vacation with her family, Shannon seduced Dane. And by the end of the school year, Agnes wasn't Dane's girlfriend, anymore.

4

Maybe it's the Irish blood. Dane's got both Irish and Scottish flowing through his veins. Shannon is full Irish. Her father Aaron can speak Gaelic, and her mother Lindy is fresh off the boat. Her older sister Rowen is the image of their mom. Molly is the youngest and looks like Shannon.

Whatever it was, it hit Dane like a ton of bricks. It seemed like all Shannon had to do was take off her pants one time, and he was completely entranced by her.

He told me, "Bro, the second I came in that pussy, it was as if my whole being had dissolved inside of her, and now she keeps me in there like a little magic box."

All I could see was that this poor guy was more in love than he'd ever been before. He was a goner. It was as though a part of him had disappeared inside of her. When I looked at him, I could almost see through him, like his spirit had left his body and gone to heaven. I don't know if Shannon and Dane were a perfect match, like I'd thought him to be with Agnes, but I do admit the two of them looked good together.

Dane's music was really beginning to take off at this point. During the summer, his band Maelstrom began playing the fireman's fair circuit, and he and I started playing at coffee houses, as an acoustic duo. We called ourselves Fingerpickin' Good, it wasn't long before we secured a steady gig at a place called Muddy Cup. It was the hippest coffee shop in the area and it actually did enough business on Friday nights that they can afford to pay us. Our repertoire was mostly covers of classic rock bands with a little blues and country mixed in. The owner was an old hippie, who really liked us.

During this time, Shannon became devotedly supportive of Dane. She encouraged him to write his own songs, and was always by his side. She became his muse. Sara and I accompanied them on every adventure. We all loved the outdoors, so we did a lot of camping and kayaking together. Sara and Shannon even began to bond, but as always, Sara pushed the sentiment beyond the bounds of prudence as far as Shannon was concerned, and their friendship was short lived.

Sara is bisexual. She's hit on just about every female in our circle of friends. On one particular outing, we had come back to camp from swimming, and Dane and I decided to do a little fishing. Shannon wanted to take a nap, so Sara stayed with her.

According to Shannon, Sara crawled into their tent as she was changing her clothes. As they talked, she placed her hand between Shannon's legs and began to massage her cootch. According to Shannon, she pushed her away and told her to leave.

Sara's version is a little different. She says that Shannon did try to stop her, at first, but as she persisted Shannon became wet in seconds, and was so turned on that when she pushed Sara away, she crawled between her legs and licked her pussy first.

It was a case of she says, and she says, and Dane and I thought it was hilarious. All it did was widen the rift between the two girls. But I know Sara. She may be a lot of things, but she's not a liar. She's not afraid of anyone. I've never heard her say anything behind anyone's back that she won't say to their face. She's cunning enough to see the big picture, and willing enough to let people bury themselves.

. . . . .

Sara wasn't Shannon's only problem. She is very insecure and very jealous of any girl who talks to Dane, especially his ex-girlfriends. She constantly accuses him of cheating, which is too bad, because he tells me that he's never been unfaithful to her during the times they've been officially together. I have no reason to disbelieve him.

They say that friends make the best lovers, but I always say, if you want to end a friendship with someone, fall in love with them. Cause when the love affair ends, and they always do, you can't be friends anymore. At least you can't hang out in the same circles where a new lover has taken your place.

In Shannon's world, ex-girlfriends are definitely not to be tolerated, and even casual female friends are a no-no, which is also bad for her because she doesn't have many friends to begin with. To most, she immediately comes off as being cold. She seems to dislike people before she even gets to know them. And she seems to be intent on keeping Dane insulated in her little world of two.

I could see her point when it came to Agnes. She hadn't completely given up on Dane, and during the first few months of our senior year, it was plain to see that she was constantly trying to seduce him back from Shannon. She did it for the whole audience to see during the marching band's halftime show one September Friday night.

As Dane was coming forward centerfield, playing his opening guitar solo, Agnes glided past, directly behind him and said something into his ear. Dane smiled, I saw it, Sara saw it, and Shannon saw it. Everyone saw it, but to most, it was just part of the show.

Later, Dane told me that she said, "Meet me after the game."

Of course, he didn't meet her, and later that evening, I saw how far someone can fall after all of their dreams have been shattered.

That night after the game, everyone kind of split up and went their own way. Dane and Shannon spent the evening at his house with his parents, which Sara and I were invited to. Sara didn't want to go, so we hung out at another soiree and got smashed. By midnight, Sara was drunk and bored and ready to leave, when Agnes walked into the party.

She found us right away, and began to sob on my shoulder, completely ignoring Sara, which then, of course, automatically pissed her off. So Sara, gets the bright idea to get Agnes hammered and seduce her. I felt bad for her, but she did look good in the flowery sun dress and cowboy boots she was wearing, and in the mood I was in, it didn't seem like a bad idea at all. Agnes was already halfway pissed, and had come there to finish herself off.

Two or three beers later, she excused herself, and wandered off into the backyard to take a leak. After a few minutes, we followed her outside, and found her down by the fence line that bordered the property. She was just finishing her pee when she saw us coming. She quickly stood up and crossed her arms in front of herself to keep warm. As we came closer, I noticed that her dress kept lifting in the wind, giving me a nice view of her pink colored panties.

Sara threw me a really fiendish glance, and said, "Let's have some fun with her."

My dick was already hard.

Agnes leaned on the fence and gazed out into the tree line, as if she hadn't noticed we were there.

Sara sidled up to her and in an almost convincingly concerned tone she asked, "Ohh, Honey... Are you okay?"

And then she gave me the nod to make my move.

Agnes looked straight ahead as she answered her.

"I hate that bitch..." she began to say, but before she could finish, I had come up behind her, and wrapped my arms around her. She didn't move, but I could swear that I'd heard a sigh escape her lips.

"Ohh, I know," Sara assured her. "I don't understand what he sees in that shameless hussy."

She began to nod at me more urgently.

I lifted Agnes' dress, pressing myself against her. To my surprise, she pulled her panties aside, inviting me. I squeezed her breasts as I entered her, her nipples standing erect in the grasp of my warm and wandering hands. As I began to thrust in and out of her, I could hear my belly making dull slapping sounds against the cool softness of her cotton covered behind. Sara leaned in, and pushed her tongue into Agnes' mouth.

At first, she just let us do what we wanted, and didn't react much at all. I figured she would just let us have our way with her, until it was over. But when Sara slid her hand up her thigh, and against her clit, she began to meet my thrusts, and within minutes, she started to come. Her knees buckled, and as I was about to give her what for and let myself go, Sara shoved me away from her.

"Not yet, Don Juan," she cooed, and then she lowered her own pants, and kicked them aside.

She pulled Agnes' panties down and pushed her to the ground, which wasn't very hard to do. Sara spread Agnes' legs and began to lick her thighs.

"Me now, Joshua," she ordered.

So, I knelt down behind her and pushed myself in.

Agnes soon began to come, again, and when she did, Sara climaxed. When my partner starts to come, that's what usually sends me over the edge, but two girls achieving orgasm together, that was outta sight! Leave it to Sara to come up with a plan that had involved a simultaneous triple cumfest.

All three of us were wrecked, but needless to say, Agnes didn't like Sara, or me very much, after that, and she pretty much had given up on Dane, as well. But Shannon, on the other hand, would never let Agnes out of her sight for very long.

. . . . .

For Halloween, Dane held a costume party at the farm. First up was a haunted hayride that wound around the property, and ended up at a bonfire in the middle of a cornfield. A fairly elaborate soiree, we had spent the day installing porta-potties at the site and scary stuff along the trail. The property has been owned by the Bruckner family since the 1750's. There is an old family cemetery along the trail that contains graves dating back to that time, which in the dark of the night is spooky enough. We had a few guys jump out from behind the old tombstones and scare everyone.

Most attendees had worked hard on their costumes. One couple, Bobby Whitlock and Nayelene Stratton came as the Blues Brothers. Complete with the suits, hats, and cheap sunglasses, they had also dyed their faces and hands blue. At first, no one recognized them. Of course, there were enough witches, ghosts, ghouls, and goblins to film a tenth sequel of *Night of the Living Dead*. By the time the party had kicked into high gear, makeup had begun to smear, parts of costumes had disappeared, and most of the characters had assumed a general appearance of dishevelment that made them look the part.

Despite the fancy facilities, whenever nature would call, most people simply slipped away into the darkness to water the cornfield. At some point late in the evening, I'd staggered off to take my turn. A few yards into the foliage I discovered a trail of discarded clothing, so I followed it, until it got down to boxers, bra, and panties, and then I stumbled into the Blues Couple, who were in the middle of taking a roll through the corn, and from the way it appeared, they were about to arrive at their destination.

The part I found fascinating was that with their clothing removed, it was apparent that not only had they dyed their faces and hands blue, but they had covered their whole bodies as well.

I don't think they noticed me, being preoccupied and all, so, I tip-toed away and found a place to pee. As I began to finally relieve myself, I started to think about the blue sex people, and I thought to myself, *What better time than now, to give Sluggo a good back rub?*

When I'd finished pampering the dog, I looked around, and in my inebriated bliss, I started walking in what turned out to be the wrong direction. At some point I came to the conclusion that I was lost. It was dark. I couldn't even see the glow of the bonfire. So, I kept walking, figuring that this garden on steroids had to end somewhere.

"Hmm, this is quite the conundrum," I thought out loud.

I find myself in quite the pickle.

But soon enough, I found the perimeter, which came out onto the road in front of Dane's house. Only I still didn't know where I was, because I was down the road a ways, and totally wasted.

Suddenly, I heard a racket coming from my left, and I saw a couple of guys bashing in a mailbox with baseball bats. Not even considering that they might turn the bats on me, I walked right up to them to get a closer look at this random act of stupidity.

I asked them if they knew where Dane lived, and they didn't seem to know, but they asked me if I needed a ride, and also not thinking of my health, I accepted. Where I was going, I did not know, but after driving a short distance, the guys in the back seat with me began to pound my head in. I believe I managed to land a few punches myself, and then the next thing I knew, I was being shoved out of the car, while it was still moving.

I ended up in a ditch on the side of the road. When Dane and Shannon found me they were astonished, but not surprised, since somehow I had managed to wind up right in front of Dane's house.

I asked where Sara was, and Shannon told me that when she had gone into the cornfield to pee, "I saw Sara, getting her brains fucked out by your cousin Brent. I think she left with him."

I could almost hear a genuine tone of concern in her voice.

Good for them. I thought. *I was hoping that somebody might have had as much fun as I did tonight.*

. . . . .

That Christmas was the first year that Dane and I were both in solid relationships with women. So, of course, we had to indoctrinate the girls in our holiday ritual of watching the *Charlie Brown Christmas* special and the movie *It's A Wonderful Life*. Romance was the theme of that season, and since the four of us had just begun to really fall in love with our respective mates, there was plenty to go around.

It was also the season that Sally got sick, and left the store. To take up the slack, I began to work her shifts on top of mine, the result being that I found myself rolling in dough. So naturally, everyone found something good under the tree from Santa.

I found Dane a really nice used Martin Dig acoustic plug in guitar, that became his number one instrument for our gigs. Sara seemed jealous. I guess she thought that I'd picked the half-carat diamond earrings, the clothes, and the laptop I'd given her from a tree. I'm sorry my dear, that I couldn't afford to buy you a Mercedes at that point in my life.

It was that Christmas that I began to supply Shannon with enough books, DVD's, and music to last her a lifetime. It was something that we shared in common in that we both loved to read. We'd already begun to spend many an evening discussing our favorite authors' works, most of the time, while Dane serenaded us on guitar, or worked on one of the recordings he'd made.

That made Sara jealous, too. It was one thing that she blamed Shannon for keeping her from getting to Dane, but now she was occupying much of my attention as well. I was in love with Sara, and she knew it, but it bothered her that Shannon and I were able to connect on levels that she could never compete on. She knew that the only thing that was keeping me interested in her was her pussy. She knew that Shannon had a pussy, too.

. .   .   .

By springtime everyone was beginning to come down with graduation fever, and by the time that day had arrived, we had just found out that Sara was pregnant. We kept it a secret long enough that she was to walk across the stage and receive her diploma, but while most of our friends were hosting graduation parties, Sara and I were planning our wedding reception.

Sara's parents gave us a honeymoon at Conneaut Lake Resort. When we made love that night, Sara looked radiant. The time we spent together those couple of days, just the two of us, felt calm and peaceful. Sara was afraid to go on a couple of the rides at the amusement park thinking it could hurt the baby. I laughed at her. I was really looking forward to having that kid.

The hotel had been damaged in a fire and for years the place had been closed. It had only, recently been re-opened, and there were stories of doors opening and closing, on their own, disembodied voices, and the apparition of a little boy, that is said to be seen on a stairwell, chasing his ball.

The second night we were there Sara, heard the sound of a woman crying, softly. On our third and last night, I saw the boy. When he saw me, he turned and ran down the hall and around a corner. I followed him, but he seemed to have disappeared into thin air. When I told the girl at the front desk about it the next morning, she said there had been no families with kids staying in the hotel at the moment.

She said, "What you saw was a ghost, my friend."

. . . . .

It was less than a month later, that Sara lost the baby. It was all too much. Her mom breaking her leg, the spirit of the weeping woman, the anonymous little boy running away from me at the hotel, and now our child had left us, too. Too many negative vibes. My mother and Liz had come to the wedding, but my father was a no show. Sara didn't care for Liz much. It didn't help when she caught us outside under a tree, and Liz on her knees trying to straighten the crotch of my pants with her mouth.

It was over in the blink of an eye. I think at that point, Sara was already done. Still, she was willing to play the happy married couple for a few more months. To most we looked happy. We never said a cross word to each other in front of anybody. So, like us, Dane and Shannon were ready to try the life of domestic bliss themselves. When Dane proposed to her, Shannon quickly accepted.

In July, we helped them move into one of the houses that Dane's father owns. Mr. Bruckner isn't just a farmer. He's a businessman, and very wealthy. You couldn't tell by looking at him. He always wears the same work clothes, and he always has a small half smoked cigar hanging out of his mouth, that never seems to be lit.

The man is laid back, but he knows what he's doing. Sometimes, I think he portrays himself as a hayseed to lull people he's dealing with into a false sense of having the upper hand, until after they sign the papers, and realize they've been snookered.

Mr. Bruckner is part owner of several businesses, and invests in the stock market. He's into real estate. He owns property, buildings, and houses everywhere. He owns a landscaping company, which upon his graduation, he gave to Dane to run.

He didn't give Dane the house, but he sold it to him for far less than it's worth. The reason being is that he wants Dane to learn what it's like to work for something. He wants him to learn what it's like to deal with banks, run a business and a household, and honor debt. Dane has got his dad's blood in him. He's gonna be alright.

The only thing I inherited from my dad's DNA is a family history of drug addiction, alcohol abuse, suicide, and depression. He never taught me anything, or posed any kind of example, because I never really knew him. You might be inclined to think that the reason that I speak of him in the past tense is because I've never spent much time with him, which is a valid assumption, but actually we'll never get that chance, because on the second day of November, the Day Of The Dead, two days after my wife announced her intentions to divorce me, we received the news that my father had been killed in an automobile accident.

5

My dad had not made a will, but according to Liz, his wishes were to be cremated. Since he had no life insurance, and had used all of his money for his research, she was more than happy to take the cheapest route possible. That route began with a flight to Savannah, Georgia, on which she was accompanied by my mother and myself. Sara had decided that there was no time like the present to start her life without me, so she politely declined.

Upon arrival in Savannah, things got weird fast. We were met at the airport by my dad's sister Lee Ann, who had recently moved there with her husband Wayne. She was glad to meet my mother and me, but she was not happy to see Liz.

She hadn't seen or spoken to Liz in years, but apparently she'd seen my father, and apparently the word discreet was not in Lee Ann's vocabulary. She pulled Liz aside and I began to hear words like, whore, slut, sick, and depraved. Liz could not get a word in edge wise, and was soon reduced to tears.

Aunt Lee Ann was still reciting adjectives, when Liz stormed off toward the ladies room, my mother in tow.

Completely confused, I walked over to my aunt and said, "I think that went well, don't you?"

She was not amused, but she could tell by the look on my face that I was clueless. She invited me to stay with her and Uncle Wayne, and the promise of a home cooked meal made it an easy decision. I knew Liz and my mom would stay at a hotel anyway, so I accepted. I found my mother and Liz, and made a plan to meet in the morning.

Later that evening, Aunt Lee Ann told me the story. At some point, my father had gone to visit his sister for the first time in many years. He told her everything about his life since they'd last seen each other. He told her about me, and he told her all about Liz. It turns out that my dad's father and Liz's father were brothers. I say were, because they've both been dead for years, and according to Aunt Lee Ann, it's a good thing, because if they weren't, my father and Liz would be.

Neither my dad nor Liz had ever mentioned this to me. I guess they felt that my mother and I weren't on the need to know list. I can understand their reasons. It's no big deal to me, anyway. I don't see anything wrong with it. I didn't tell Aunt Lee Ann that, though. Apparently, she can't get behind that whole first cousin, sex and marriage thing.

She had one more thing to tell me, or should I say show me, before we went to bed. We went out to the garage, and in it sat a 1967 Chevy van, in pristine condition, and inside of it, were some of the nicest guitars I'd ever seen.

"It's all yours," she explained. "It's all he left ya. It's all he had to leave ya."

Wait 'till Dane sees this. He's gonna come himself.

· · · · ·

In the morning, my mother, Liz, and I met with the mortician to make arrangements to have my father's remains reduced to ash. Afterwards, we went to meet with his investigative partner, Phil Parsons, who began by telling us what he knew about the accident. Since the details of my father's entire life, border on the bizarre, what he had to say was not all that surprising.

Just the same, it was chilling for me to hear, because it made me question whether the man had indeed possessed the capabilities to interact with the dead or was it simply that he happened to be going insane.

Apparently, as he lay dying in the hospital, he had regained consciousness long enough to tell Phil, that as he was driving away from the grounds of the estate that they had been investigating, something unknown took over the wheel and the accelerator of his car, and sent it speeding out of control. Then from out of nowhere, Selena, the knife wielding ex-girlfriend, turned succubus, stepped into his path, causing him to swerve, and slam head on into a tree.

Once Liz had heard the details of my father's accident, she had no further interest in hearing anything else. She and my mother went sight seeing, or shopping, or whatever, just as long as she didn't have to continue the meeting with Phil, or Beth Ferguson, who had joined us mid-story, and who Liz had no desire to see.

Phil got me up to speed on the origins of the case, and then he began to show me some of the evidence they'd recorded. Some of the video footage was hard for Beth to watch, and she had to leave the room. I was impressed with the amount of documentation they had gathered on this case, alone. I asked Phil to make me copies of everything, and send it to me, so I could study the rest of it at home.

He agreed to do it for me, and added, "Keep an open mind, son… It's in your veins."

. . . . .

A few weeks later, I received the material, and in my spare time, I began to go through it. Even though I've had my own experiences, I'm still a skeptic when it comes down to someone else's word. I have to admit that this stuff was pretty convincing. Even Dane and Shannon watched some of it with me.

We've done a little of our own amateur ghost hunting, and they agree that compared to what we do, my father and his friends have seen the real deal.

. . . . .

They arrived early in the day and began to unpack and set up their equipment all over the house. Each room was equipped with Hi8, night vision, infrared, and full spectrum cameras, which were also equipped with infrasound audio capability. The team members split up into pairs and began a baseline sweep of the entire place to check for any electromagnetic fields that are believed to indicate the presence of spiritual energy.

Aside from a few noises and a door slamming shut, not much happened during the daylight hours. They did manage to pick up a few high readings on the EMF meters, but those could easily be explained away by a house full of old and out of code electrical wiring.

At dinner, the team, which consisted of my father and Phil Parsons, investigators Beth Ferguson and Scott LaFarve, medium Susan Vance, and equipment technician Clarence Mumford, went over the plans for the initial night investigation. As they discussed the details of who would cover each part of the house, EVP experts Mark Matheson and his wife June, arrived.

Now, that everyone was together, my father was finally able to tell the story of the Stone family and the house, in which within its walls, they are still believed to live, and within its halls, they are still believed to walk.

. . . . .

Winter Winds was built by Doctor Wilhelm Stone. It was completed in 1858, about three years before the start of the Civil War. Just outside the city limits of Savannah, Georgia, the name seems an odd choice, considering the sultry southern locale.

But by all accounts, once one steps over the threshold, and into the front hall, they are to find nothing sultry about the place. In fact, once they reach the room in which Wilhelm Stone, and his wife Petula once slept, the heart of the house, they find it to be almost unbearably cold.

Wilhelm and Petula had three children. A son, Jacob, and two daughters, Temperance and Prudence. About the time that Prudence, the youngest of the three had reached the age of twelve, Stone left home to join the South in the war, as a field medic.

By the time he'd returned home, their son Jacob had died of yellow fever. A year later, Prudence died when, while riding with some friends, she fell from her horse and was impaled by the blade of a farm implement. Within months Petula had fallen into an irreversible depression, and was found hanging from the upstairs balcony. Then, as if some unseen nemesis had been bent on tearing Stone's whole family from him, Temperance succumbed to injuries she'd suffered when their carriage flipped, and she and her father were thrown to the ground.

From then on, Stone, distraught with grief, became a bitter man. He tried to press on, and even remarried. He switched his practice from general medicine to psychiatry and was known for using hypnosis in the treatment of his patients. But the loss of his family continued to eat away at him, and he became abusive to his wife. She eventually left him, alone in the house, and he eventually shot himself.

Those who have occupied the house have reported hearing and seeing all of the members of the Stone family. There are also accounts of being touched, and especially women being caressed and fondled as they lay in bed at night. Some have even claimed to have detected the scent of a woman's sex and to having experienced an overwhelming feeling of sexual arousal.

While footsteps have been heard, objects have been moved, and doors have opened and closed, no one up to the point of my father's investigation had been seriously harmed. But on the first night they spent in the house, that was about to change.

．　．　．　．　．

On Susan's walk, she claims to having interacted with Stone's wife Petula and his daughter Temperance. She attempted to make contact with Stone himself, but she said that his spirit was very powerful, and he would not speak with her.

Susan revealed that Petula Stone committed suicide, because once the children had matured, her husband began to ignore her intimately, and turned his attention to the girls. The guilt that she was powerless to stop him had consumed her.

Susan's conversation with Temperance was even more astounding. She claimed that the girl told her that she and her sister had both had sex with their father, many times. She also said that she and her sister began to have sex, together. Her final revelation put the pudding in the pie. Temperance, whose spirit was still that of a fourteen year old girl, let it be known that she had been four months pregnant with her father's child at the time of her death.

Later in the evening, Mark and June captured two EVP's, which seem to confirm Susan's findings.

They had asked the question, "If there is someone here with us, what is your name?"

Upon playback, you can clearly hear a girl's voice reply, "My name is Temperance Stone."

When they asked the question, "Why are you not at rest?" they were stunned by the answer.

"Because I'm pregnant."

As if that wasn't enough, several cameras filmed an orb moving all over the house. Inside the orb was a smaller orb, that led everyone to agree that they might possibly have witnessed the partially formed apparition of the spirit of Temperance Stone and her baby.

All of the evidence they'd gathered up to that point, would have been enough to call it an outstanding night's work, but the spirits of Winter Winds were only just getting started.

At about 3:00 in the morning, as Mark and June were descending the main staircase, Mark was shoved with enough force to send him tumbling down the steps, and on to the floor of the front hall. Besides being knocked unconscious, he received a broken jaw, several bruised ribs, and a broken leg. It was as if Wilhelm Stone, in meting out punishment for bothering his daughter, had attempted to help Mark down the steps, and out the front door of his house.

Then, it became apparent that Stone meant to keep the intruders of his house from recovering once and for all.

In the master bedroom, Beth and Susan heard something off in the distance. As if it was coming from another realm, or dimension.

Beth whispered, "What was that?"

"He's coming," Susan replied.

"Who?" Beth asked, almost sure that she didn't want to know.

Susan hesitated for a moment, as if trying to be certain, "Stone... Stone is coming."

They began to hear whispering.

"It's starting," she continued, her voice trembling.

The walls began to heave and pulsate, to and fro, as one's chest would in breathing heavily. The whispering evolved into moaning and whimpering. Quietly, at first, and then progressively louder, they began to hear the sound of heavy breathing, and they realized they were listening to someone having sex.

Beth murmured, "What the fuck?!"

She began to feel strange, her own breathing becoming labored. She began to feel flush, and in a matter of seconds, she could feel herself becoming aroused.

She looked over at Susan, who had already lowered her pants, and cried, "What's happening...?"

But before she could finish the sentence, she had slid her hand into her own pants to discover that she had become completely soaked.

Everything inside of her tried to fight it, but it was as if some unseen force had drained her of her will. She penetrated herself and began to masturbate, feverishly. Susan approached her, and the two women immediately began to tear at each other's clothing, ultimately engaging in a relentless sexual bond, licking, sucking, and fingering, until they both began to come, so violently that when it passed, neither one of them could regain their composure, until when almost a half an hour later, the others had found them lying naked on the floor.

It was determined later, that Stone was able to place the two of them under some kind of hypnosis, causing them to simultaneously lose control of their inhibitions. The most fascinating element to the event was that he left them both aware of what they were doing, and unable to stop themselves.

But whatever they had surmised, above all else, it was determined that it was not safe to remain inside the walls of Winter Winds, a moment longer. They packed their equipment and left the house quickly, before Wilhelm Stone could unleash any more hell that he undoubtedly still had waiting for them.

. . . . .

Thanks to the magic of film, I was able to view the footage from my father's final investigation, and thanks to Beth and Susan, I had become compelled to do something about the erection that the vision of their paranormal peep show had bestowed upon me. I'm not sure if ghost hunting is in my blood, as Phil had hoped, but I do know that what's in my veins had rushed to Sluggo's head, and had left him feeling warm and cozy all over. He wasn't scared stiff, but he was definitely stiff.

While I was intrigued by some of the most irrefutable evidence that I had ever seen, of malevolent spiritual forces in action, I was even more interested in the actions of the two women, especially because I had believed that they would have eventually hooked up, anyway.

At least, that's what I had wanted to believe. As the two of them moved about the house, I followed them with the lens of my eyes almost exclusively trained on their rear ends, all the while pulling for them to become startled, embrace, and then suddenly realize that there was no better time than that moment to bury their faces in each other's frightened figs.

The way it went down had more than exceeded my wildest expectations, and I'll be "studying" that clip for some time to come. I might not be a ghost buster like my father, but I do have one of his traits coursing through my veins, and it'll probably be the one that gets me in the most trouble.

6

I should get started on that letter to Sara. I'm sure the story will thoroughly bore her, but there are some moments. It's just a script from your typical soap opera, and you know how soap operas are. You can miss months at a time and still know what's going on.

It all really started when Dane and Shannon moved to Gettysburg. Dane had decided to take a course in audio engineering. He'd considered a school in Arizona, but the school in Gettysburg was a good one, and it seemed to be a more accessible option. Besides that, Shannon didn't want to move so far from home.

I knew they had a lot of stuff to move, and I also knew that Dane would want to have his favorite guitars and equipment close to him. He had been in the market for a van, since his trusty Subaru Forester had finally begun to give out on him, so I gave him the van that I'd inherited from my dad, and I threw in a nice Martin D45 acoustic guitar for good luck. Dane almost did come himself.

Anyway, we got everything down there, and got them settled in. I actually spent the next several weekends with them. I like Gettysburg. I feel like it's a place where I belong. I can feel the history, and I can almost swear that I've lived there before, in another life. Dane feels the same way. The problem is, that aside from the quaint historic atmosphere, there's not much going on. Unless of course, you happen to be looking for spirits. In Gettysburg, they say the whole town is haunted. If you ask, the locals will tell you that you can probably find a ghost in every corner. But why ask? It took but one night in their new home for Dane and Shannon to discover that they were not alone. Shannon in particular, was not happy with the idea that she would be sharing her home with someone that she could not see.

Despite her weariness of her unwanted roommates, Shannon immersed herself in making their new house a home. She spent hours in the shops that surround the town square, and enjoyed filling the place with her personal touch.

Dane had his studio upstairs, and since he's not the tidiest person in the world, the space quickly became a disaster area. Shannon stayed out, preferring to leave his chaotic organizational methods to him, alone. Well, actually, she left it to him and their pet rabbit, which he let run loose. Of course, it chewed up everything in sight, including the cables to his equipment. Dane loves animals. He couldn't wrap his head around the idea of imprisoning his little friend in a cage, despite the fact that it was systematically chewing his house from its frame.

·　·　·　·　·

They still hadn't set a wedding date, but I really thought that Dane and Shannon were it. They seemed to be a perfect match, and I had become convinced that they were meant for each other. But after the move, I began to notice trouble in paradise.

I saw Dane begin to pick at her, playfully at first. Then, it started turning mean. He even started to do it in front of other people, which caused her a fair amount of humiliation and embarrassment. I could see Shannon losing her spirit, and becoming withdrawn, right before my eyes. I knew they weren't gonna last the way they were going.

One evening, during a really bad argument, Shannon stormed out of the house. Dane wasn't impressed. So, I followed her outside, and caught up with her a few blocks down the street. We continued down the sidewalk for a while in silence, and when we finally stopped, we were at the steps of a pub. Romney's Cork, read the sign. I suggested that we ought to get a beer.

Once inside, I did most of the talking. I told her to hang in there, that Dane would grow up, sooner or later, and that she should be patient. I told her that the two of them looked good together.

She began to cry, of course, and she told me, "Looks aren't everything," but she promised to take my advice.

She said that she wasn't gonna let Dane get away that easy, and when we got back to the house, she hugged me, and said, "Thanks."

After that, she began to lean on me with all of her problems.

Later, I asked Dane why he was doing it to her. He isn't normally one to discuss affairs of the heart, so I wasn't surprised when he didn't answer me. I pressed my luck, and told him that he was screwing up. He just tuned me out. I didn't say much more. Who was I to tell him what to do, especially since I was already divorced.

. . . . .

It was around that time, when Eugene hired a new girl down at the store. Her name is Gina Sutherland and in the few weeks she'd been there, we'd already developed an uneasy alliance with each other. I say uneasy, because she spent most of her time avoiding work, and looking good at it. I just prayed that she wouldn't get fired. She was good for business. Men started coming to the store just to hit on her. She flirted with all of them.

I didn't mind that she didn't get much work done. I spent a lot of my time following her around with my dick wagging. Her luscious behind made any pair of jeans she wore look as though they were made only for her. There was an immediate attraction between the both of us, purely physical at the moment, but our connection had been pretty innocent up to this point.

I had to listen to Gina snivel and complain about an endless string of boyfriends, so what else is new, all the while feigning concern and pretending to care for her only as a friend. Sounds like a pattern, doesn't it? She would return my attention subtly or not so subtly teasing me with her very unsubtle feminine wiles.

This game of push and pull occurred when Gina could sense that I was becoming annoyed with her lack of interest in doing her job. Her wardrobe mostly consisted of low cut tops and mini skirts, and always at just the moment she would suspect that I was about to let her have it, she would bend over or spread her legs just enough to give me a peek at what was barely covered by her underwear.

She told me that on several nights a week, she worked in a "gentleman's club." At first, I thought she meant as a bartender or a waitress. I'm not dumb, but I've known her since she was fourteen or fifteen. She is the stepdaughter of a state police detective. So, when she told me that she was a dancer, I wasn't shocked, but I was a little surprised. What tantalized me the most was the nonchalant and cavalier way she expressed herself. The idea sent my imagination running wild.

Gina used to be a cheerleader. I could still see her smiling proudly at the top of the pyramid at football games. I wondered how, in just a little more than a year, she could evolve from that, to slithering down a pole in front of a bunch of drunk and horny slobs. But I'm no angel, and somehow, I just couldn't erase the picture in my mind, of her sliding down my pole in that cheerleader outfit.

.   .   .   .   .

Dane and Shannon were now fighting all the time. She didn't like any of his friends, especially girlfriends. Her jealousy had escalated beyond belief. She began to accuse him of cheating on her, constantly. She was miserable around everyone. At gatherings, she would sit apart from everyone and sulk.

We played a gig in Gettysburg at a coffee house called The Velvet Underground. Our friend Kelly Lynne McCrea, had come down with me to hang out and see the show. Shannon accused Dane of talking to Kelly Lynne all night and ignoring her. Depending on how you wanted to look at it, that might have been true.

Anyway, it got to the point where it became almost unbearable to hang out with the two of them. You almost couldn't be in the same room with them, at times. The tension was so thick you could cut it with a knife, and they almost couldn't discuss anything without getting into a pissing match. I had to get up and leave several times, and once, I just packed my things, and drove home.

It's funny how when two people first fall in love, neither of them can do anything wrong. Everything is hunky-dory and lovey-dovey, and we are completely blind to any fault our partner may have. Then as time goes on, the temporary mental illness that we call being in love wears off, and at some point, we begin to notice all those things that bother us about them, and we begin to voice our displeasure in it.

Towards the end, affectionate pet names like babe and sweetheart, are replaced by mean names like, bitch and asshole, and it seems like nothing either one of those same two people can do is right. Dane and Shannon were those two people. I knew that it wouldn't be long.

7

I feel like I really got to know Shannon for the first time on the drive home from Gettysburg. She had decided that she and Dane needed to take some time apart, and he saw no reason to argue. The problem was that Shannon didn't own a car at the time, and Dane refused to help her get home. I got the call.

Naturally, we talked the whole way back. She told me her life story, at least what she had so far in her twenty years on earth, and I in turn told her mine. She complained that all of her friends had turned on her. She couldn't understand why Dawn Marie had abandoned her during the time Dane was seeing Gabrielle. It wasn't long before I realized that this was going to be Shannon's version of life, which meant that she was little red riding hood, and everyone else was the big bad wolf.

She said that she couldn't talk to her parents. I got that she blamed her mother for something, and I sensed there was some kind of issue with her dad. According to Shannon, she didn't even get along with her older sister Rowen, and she didn't have a lot of good things to say about her. A little jealousy about something, maybe? The part about her family was perplexing to me, because on the outside they seemed as close as a family could get.

Most of what she told me didn't seem to add up. One thing had quickly become apparent, though. Shannon didn't seem to get along with anybody, and one by one, she was basically dumping everyone from her life. As the conversation progressed I did come to the realization that she wasn't telling me everything.

Of course, she complained about her relationship with Dane. She said that she was sure that all of his old girlfriends were trying to get into his pants, especially Gabrielle Swanson.

"And now, even Dawn Marie is after him," she sniveled, "probably just to screw with me. I can't trust any of them. I hate them. Dane wants me to hang out with them. Why should I hang out with someone I don't like?"

She had a point, but that's what is tough about that whole friendship thing, after people break up. I told Shannon that I agreed with her, but then I got cheeky and played the devil's advocate. I told her that now, she was the ex-girlfriend, and by her principles, she was not going to be able to hang out with Dane, if he meets someone else.

She went on.

"Dane expects me to be his friend, his lover, and his mother, all at the same time. One minute he's a man, and the next minute he's a little boy. He expects everything from me, and hardly ever gives in return. He thinks fucking me is the way to give."

She told me that she was tired of being the one that gives. Everyone wants her to give. Everyone has always wanted her to give.

My question was, "Who was everyone?"

This was when I began to realize that Shannon had issues beyond the realm of normalcy. Deep seated, hidden issues that no one knew about. The problem was, at that point, she wasn't tellin'.

What she did tell me was that she had decided a few weeks before, to shut Dane off. What she meant was that she'd made her pussy off limits, until he decided to get his act together. The first thing I thought was, that's not gonna be good for anyone. But as I glanced down between the legs of those skimpy, sexy, tight white shorts she was wearing, I began to wonder if it might somehow be good for me. Within seconds, Sluggo was thinking the same thing.

Still, I managed to keep a grip and I tried to explain to her that men need sex. Not just for fun, but as a way to let off steam. I told her that guys need to come at least every other day, because of hormonal pressure that builds up inside of them. I said that's why it seems like we are always horny.

Of course, I added that when we are with a beautiful girl, especially if we're in love with that girl, it makes it fun and easy to relieve that pressure by making love with them.

"It is a way for us to express our feelings," I said. "That's why we're always chasing you girls around, pokin' ya in the butt with our dicks."

The conversation had begun to shift, and even Shannon seemed to lighten up and enjoy it. It got kind of graphic, and when Shannon started to tell me some of the things that get her pussy wet, I could swear that I could feel the heat coming from between her legs. It took all I had not to put my hand in there. I thought seriously about asking her if she wanted to finish the conversation in a motel room, and when we did finally stop for a food break, I had to relieve some of that pressure we'd been talking about by hand.

Shannon spent even more time in the ladies' room. As I waited for her, I began to work myself up into another lather thinking how, between our conversation, and enforcing her no sex rule with Dane, she had probably begun to get a little pent up herself, and now, she was in there quietly putting out the fire that had been slowly burning deep inside of her. Suddenly, I could kick myself for not suggesting that room.

. . . . .

I had begun to look forward to my shifts with Gina, both mesmerized and weary of the torture she was putting me through. The more she teased me, the more I wanted to find out what she looked like, and tasted like, and felt like underneath her clothes.

What I didn't realize was, that for all the lonely times that I'd begun to spend thinking about her, and giving Sluggo a bone, it was she who couldn't sleep some nights after being near me that day, until she treated her hungry fig to some finger pie.

At least, I wouldn't have known that juicy piece of information, until she made a point of telling me. Of course, that made a point in the crotch of my pants, and then that was the point when something had to give. The point being that it was time for the clothes to come off.

I was busy storing cases of an order that had come in that day, under the deli case, when I noticed a customer waiting at the register. I looked over at Gina, and shook my head. As usual, she was sitting on a stool at the end of the counter, filing her nails.

"Can you give me a hand?!" I yelled, more of a command, than a question.

"Sure," she replied, annoyed that I'd interrupted her beauty treatment.

When she turned towards me, I noticed that the zipper of her jeans was down, she walked past me to the register, and as she did, she pushed her jeans down some exposing the top of her panties. I was sure that she had done this completely for my benefit. As she reached the register, she dropped her nail file, and squatted down to pick it up, and as she did, I could now see the crack of her lovely rear end. My cock shifted in my pants. I looked away, and continued what I was doing.

I could feel her coming toward me, and when I looked up, her crotch was in my face.

"Uhh.. not that I'm looking, but your fly is open," I stammered.

"Oh, I know… it's these stupid jeans. They always do that."

She reached down to zip them up, but I stopped her.

I tried to slip my fingers inside, but the opening was too small. I loosened the button, and as I slid my hand southward,

I realized by the dampness of her panties, that she had begun to succumb to her own mischief.

"Let's go in the back," I suggested.

"No, right here," she teased.

"We'll get caught," I pleaded.

"I know."

She was right. As I tugged at her jeans, I could hear someone starting up the front steps of the store. Gina quickly buttoned herself up, and made a beeline for the office.

I'm not done here, this can't be over. And luckily the customer only wanted a pack of smokes. I pictured Gina on the toilet, peeing the moment away, but when I got back there, she was standing in the kitchen with her hand down her pants.

"Just keepin' it warmed up for ya darlin'," she sighed.

This time, I pulled her pants down to her ankles and she stepped out of them. A pair of black lace panties was all that laid between me and the flowery jewel that I had longed for all these weeks. I knelt down, and pressed my face into her.

Gina quivered as I jabbed my tongue into the soakened fabric of her underwear. She sighed, almost impatiently, and she pushed me away. She wriggled out of her panties, and I quickly yanked my own pants down. Free of its denim prison, my shaft sprang to full mast. Gina licked her lips at the sight of it.

She squatted down in front of me, and began to lick and suckle my rod like it was an all day sucker. She was slobbering all over me, the sounds of her efforts filling the room. Her mouth felt so good that I almost started to come, so this time, I pushed her away.

As I lifted her onto the table, she whispered in my ear to hurry.

"Please, let's not get interrupted, again."

By now, her juice was running down her thigh, and her scent had begun to fill my senses like a pie on a windowsill. She grabbed my barrel and pulled me toward her split. I entered her, and began to tease her with the head of my cock.

"Hurry up!" she begged.

I pushed deeper into her, and began to let her have it. I felt my insides begin to churn, and I knew it wouldn't be long.

"We're being sooo bad," she moaned.

"I feel bad," I offered.

"Really bad," she agreed.

I was about to say something else, when Gina interrupted me.

"Joshua…" she purred.

"What?!"

"I'm gonna…"

8

Shannon and I had both been pretty open about stuff during our conversation the week before, and a few days later, I actually had begun to think that I had gone over the line. After all, she still loved Dane, and I was almost sure that it wasn't over between the two of them.

So, I wrote her a letter to apologize and to tell her not to worry about the other girls. I assured her that she was good for Dane, and that everything was gonna work out. Of course, somehow, I managed to touch on an even more sensitive issue having to do with their relationship.

In tears, she had complained to me that Dane had made a hurtful comment about the tightness of her vagina.

"He told me that he couldn't feel himself inside me!" she sniffled.

At the time, the mental picture of the dimensions of her pussy, had only served to make me hornier than I'd already been.

But now, in this letter, I was honestly trying to assure her that her genitals were fine. I explained to her that it's what all guys do when they're losing an argument with their woman. We put you down, physically, I told her ashamedly. I told her that because she had been accusing him of cheating, he'd simply retaliated by insinuating that she'd obviously been getting plenty of dick, cause her hole was the size of a cave.

A few days later, I gave her the letter. I told her that everything was gonna be okay, and not to become a stranger.

"You know where I live," I chided.

She promised to keep in touch.

· · · · ·

A few months back, my drunken neighbor Gary, to whom I affectionately refer to as Otis, had moved into the apartment to the right of mine. Quiet, he was not, and I kind of figured him out right away, when he complained that most of his utilities had tacked on large security deposits to his first billing statement.

Apparently, he'd skipped out on a few lease agreements in the past, and also wasn't very reliable at paying his bills. One evening, after only a couple months, he knocked at my door, and asked me if I knew, when the power would be fixed. I told him my electric was fine.

I asked him if he'd remembered to pay his bill, to which he replied, "They never sent me one."

I looked in his mailbox, which was full of days' worth of mail. Then, when we went into his apartment, I could see that he hadn't answered weeks of mail.

I told him, "They shut you off, because you didn't pay your bill."

He didn't even hear me.

The next thing he asks is, "Can you spot me a ten for a couple of beers?"

I knew I would never get money back from a guy who doesn't pay his debts. I felt sorry for him, but I declined.

I told him that he had a problem and, "As a friend, I'm telling you to get some help."

That's when he informed me that, "The only time I have a drinking problem, is when I'm out of money."

I couldn't argue with that logic, so I went with him down to the 'Hotel' and bought him enough drinks to sink a battleship. The only problem was that I'd had almost as much as he did to drink, and the next day I felt like there was a freight train bouncing off of the inside of my skull.

. . . . .

It happened that around the same time, a new family moved into one of the apartments downstairs. The guy was a friend of Dane's, and still is, who works at Big Red's Harley Shop, just up the road from our building. His name is Miles Holland, and his wife at that time was Ranae. They had a daughter together named Echo.

Dane knew the Hollands, both because of meeting Miles at the bike shop, and the three of them spending a lot of time riding together. Likewise, they were also into collecting guns and shooting. Dane also knew that the turnover ratio at my building was frequent, so he had suggested the place to them, before he left for Gettysburg.

Miles also raced motorcycles, which caused him to be out of town quite a bit. This in turn, allowed his very promiscuous wife to seek the comfort of other men on a regular basis. Lately, she had begun to seek that comfort upstairs at my place.

I couldn't stand Ranae, at first. She came into the store every day, and complained about everything. She never stopped talking.

No wonder the guy goes out of town so much.

She was a pain in the ass. She had a habit of turning everything anyone said into a double entendre, always sexual in nature.

She was ten years older than me, average looking, hot to trot, and she hit on me, constantly. She claimed that she and her husband had an understanding, and that they only remained together for the kid. I told her that I didn't date married women. Of course, Gina didn't like her either.

But she grew on me. Or wore me down, more likely. We both had the same views on life, and the same dark sense of humor. I actually started to like her, and before you knew it, we became friends.

It was her birthday, and Miles had actually agreed to stay home with Echo, while Ranae and I went out for a beer. We walked over to the Hotel, and twelve beers and a few shots later, we were both completely wrecked, and Ranae was all over me. I tried to resist, but I only got drunker and weaker as the night wore on.

We went outside so she could have a cigarette, and while we were out there, she grabbed my hand and shoved it down her pants, and while my hand was down her pants, I discovered that mother nature had already begun without us, and then I couldn't get her to my place fast enough.

We fooled around like that for a couple of weeks, her sneaking up to my place at night, and then tip-toeing back downstairs in the early hours, just before dawn. Finally, one weekend when Miles was out of town, and Echo was with her grandparents, Ranae was able to spend a couple of entire nights with me. As we made love on the second night, she told me that she was falling for me, and after she'd left the next day, I began to wonder what I was getting myself into.

9

It had been about a week since Shannon had left Dane in Gettysburg, and I hadn't talked to him.

On Friday morning his sister Erin called me and said, "We haven't heard from Dane, and my mother thinks you should go down there and see how he's doing."

I told Erin to tell her mother not to worry. I assured her that I'd go, and right after work I hit the road. It was the middle of rush hour, so I sat in traffic, I had plenty of time to call Dane and tell him I was coming. I didn't mention the call from Erin, I just played it like it was gonna be a random visit.

By the time I got there, I was frazzled from the drive, but Dane was cool as a cucumber. Even I had been a little worried about him, but apparently he was alright. Maybe a little too alright. I tried not to break the subject too soon, thinking maybe I'd let him bring it up. Of course, Dane doesn't like to bring anything up.

I asked him how school was going, so he led me up to his studio, and we listened to some of his work, which sounded great. Dane already had an ear for what sounds good, and he knew his way around a recording studio, but the school gave him access to the latest technology and the best equipment out there. He was in heaven.

We started to listen to some other music he was interested in, and then we grabbed a couple of guitars, and rehearsed some of our own stuff. He taught me the chords to an Irish folk song he'd written, and once I had it down, he recorded us. He said he'd add the rest of the instruments later.

I couldn't help but notice that the screen saver on his computer was a picture of a naked anime girl. Since I was interested, he showed me a few more, and then he switched to pictures of real naked girls, in various poses. Some were kinky. One shot depicted twin sisters squatting and peeing off of the edge of a huge boulder in the middle of the woods. It was Dawn Marie and Gabrielle Swanson.

I had no idea that Dane was into that kind of stuff, and I wondered when he'd found the time to do it. As he scrolled through a few more pictures of their pee soaked pussies, he explained that the Swanson sisters had moved to Maryland with their dad. As it turned out, their dad's place was just over the Maryland border, less than twenty miles from Gettysburg.

Dane continued the sexy slide show, and all of a sudden, without him saying anything, I began to see naked pictures of Shannon. There were about ten shots of her in various stages of undress that seemed to move in sequence.

The first shot showed her sitting on the bed, her denim skirt hiked up, her legs open, giving a hot view of her bush, through a pair of sheer mint green panties. In the next picture, she had removed her shirt, and had pulled her bra above her breasts, her hands raised to cover herself, and in the next, her hand lowered to allow her voyeur a glimpse of one soft pink areola and nipple.

In these first few pictures her face had reddened, and she wore the expression of someone who was being forced to do something against her will. But by the sixth or seventh shot, she looked as though a feeling of delicious lassitude had enfolded her.

In the next shot Shannon laid on the bed in a black lace bra and panties, her left arm over her face, and her right hand clearly massaging the mound between her legs. By the end of the sequence, she was naked, on her knees, her ass facing the camera, her finger inserted into her sex. You could barely see her face in this position, but her expression left no doubt in my mind that she was enjoying herself.

All couples do it. I did it with Sara. But for Dane to purposely show me these pictures, it just boggled my mind.

I said, "Dude, that's Shannon."

He said, "Yep."

I said, "Why are you showing me this?"

He said, "Now, you know what Shannon looks like naked."

And then the pictures were gone.

Then he said, "Check this out," and he flipped the screen to a picture of another hot naked girl, sitting on a 1980 Honda CB1000 custom motorcycle.

"I like that better," he smirked. "Come on, I have to show you something."

He led me downstairs, and outside to a shed in the back yard. The thought crossed my mind that he might have a couple of naked chicks stashed in there, too, but when he opened the door, I saw a beautiful black 1998 Harley Davidson Sportster Sport 1200. It had a custom black and white, two tone gas tank, six-inch handlebars, and forward mounted controls.

"Meet my new girlfriend," he beamed. "I just got her yesterday. I needed something to get around town on that gets decent gas mileage… Seventy miles per. Now, we gotta get you one."

I almost shit myself. Of course, we had to take her for a spin, and I almost shit myself again when he opened her up to about 80 mph on the way to the Harley shop. Call me insane, but Dane talked me into buying a nice sky blue 1997 Harley 883 Sportster. I had no way of getting it home, so I kept it there at Dane's, and once I was able to get my driver's permit, we'd be able to ride around Gettysburg, together.

We did eventually get around to talking about Shannon. He told me that she thought he was cheating, and that they had not had sex in months, and she didn't want him seeing Agnes or the Swanson sisters, because she hates them, and she thinks they're trying to steal him from her. All of this, of course, was old news, via Shannon.

I did say to Dane that he should be careful, because Dawn Marie and Gabrielle might just be trying to break him and Shannon up, and once they accomplish their mission, they won't want anything to do with him.

Though, I thought to myself that if he could get them to pee in the woods for him, they must enjoy his company a little. Dawn Marie is a lusty fun loving girl, who obviously doesn't mind mixing a little pleasure with the business of watching her sister's back. And Gabrielle simply follows her sister's lead as long as it offers a means to an end. The end for Gabrielle being revenge.

Dane assured me that he never cheated on Shannon while they were officially together, but that he'd had sex with all of those girls before, and after Shannon. This again, was no news to me. But he also told me in no uncertain terms that he was through with Shannon, and that he was going back to Maryland to see the Swanson sisters, and that he planned on having sex with both of them. What could I say? I bought him a big box of condoms.

10

Upon arriving back in town, I called Erin and gave my official report. I told her to tell her mom that Dane was fine. In fact, he was more than fine. He was peachy. She was grateful for the news. Before she hung up she reminded me about her graduation party in a couple of weeks. I assured her I wouldn't miss it.

As for what I thought about the naked Shannon photos, I considered that maybe Dane was giving me his blessing. After all, he had made a point of assuring me that they were through. He also made certain that I would see the engagement ring dangling from the hangman's noose in his studio.

Just the same, I tossed my hopes aside, and put it down to him hating Shannon at the time, and simply wanting to make a fool out of her. The problem was that I couldn't get those images of her out of my mind. The other problem was that she wouldn't let me.

I was in the middle of taking a shower, when she showed up at my door. I told her to wait a minute, and I put on a pair of running shorts. I was still wet when I let her in. I grabbed us a couple of beers, and I sat down next to her on the couch.

Now, she was wearing those skimpy white shorts of hers and a very revealing top. She was sitting so close to me that her knee was touching mine, and she started to go on about how she hates the Swanson sisters, and how she doesn't understand why Dane wants to be friends with them, and how she knows they're fucking him, and then she started to cry.

Of course, I melt when women cry, and the next thing she told me was that one of the reasons she thought Dane had cheated was, "Cause he's been buggin' me to shave my pussy!"

"Why don't you just do it?" I asked.

"Because I don't want to," she sniffled.

"I like a nice patch," I replied, though I don't think it even registered.

"I know why he wants me to do it, too," she continued.

"And why is that?" I asked her, honestly curious to know the answer.

"It's because Gabrielle Swanson shaves hers!"

Okay, okay, I was trying to keep a grip, but this hot chick was talking about her pussy, and now her legs were crossed on my couch, and I had a bird's eye view of her crotch, and her black panties were peeking out from the sides of her skimpy white shorts, and I knew what she looked like under those skimpy white shorts and those black panties, cause those naked pictures were still only four days fresh in my mind, and suddenly, my dick was tightening up in my shorts, and she was still talking, and all I wanted to do was get into that spot between her legs.

So, we finished, and somehow, I managed to give her some advice, which I'm sure she didn't hear, and I reassured her that I would talk to Dane, and that everything would be alright. She smiled and wiped her tears, and told me that I was really sweet, and then she stood up to leave, and she hugged me, tight, and I'm sure she could feel Sluggo, who was still aching to get off the leash, and then she left, and then I went in and took another shower.

. . . . .

Dane called to say that he'd be in town at the end of the month to DJ Erin's graduation party. I told him about Shannon's visit, well most of it, and I explained that she was trying to hold her ground, but that she desperately wanted to get back with him. His reaction was to tell me that he definitely was not ready to get back with her.

I also took the opportunity to ask him why he had made the crack about her vagina, even though I knew the answer.

"Is it really that bad?" I queried.

"Bro, please... cut me a fuckin' break."

The tone in his voice was all it took to let me know that what I had told Shannon was correct. I didn't push the subject.

About a week later, I was running on the trail behind my house. It's an old rail line, and at the point where the trail passes through each town there is a rest area equipped with a decent toilet and a water fountain.

I had stopped for a sip of cold water, and when I turned from the fountain, I saw a pretty girl riding a bicycle towards me in the distance. As she came closer, I realized that it was Shannon. She pulled up with a big smile on her face.

"Hi," she said.

I returned the greeting with, "Hi yourself... fancy meetin' you here on the trail."

Okay, not very witty, but I had been taken by surprise, mesmerized, and had found myself at a loss for words. I had already thought that Shannon was a beautiful girl, but at the moment, she had never looked more so.

Her face was flush from the sunshine and exercise. Her hair was pulled back, and once again, she was wearing very little clothing. The girl frequently goes braless and this day was no different. It was all I could do to pull my gaze away from her chest.

There was something else though. She seemed to actually be in a pleasant mood for the first time in months. The occasion was rare. Maybe the sunlight had gotten into her veins.

We talked a while, and I told her that I was pulling for her and Dane to get back together, which was a lie, but I added that if things didn't work out between them, I hoped that we could still be friends. She assured me that we would.

She brought up the letter that I'd written her, and told me that she appreciated that I cared enough to worry about her.

"I like you Joshua… and I like talking to you."

When she smiled, I melted.

"Anytime," I assured her.

We said our goodbyes, and as she continued on down the trail, I watched her, until she disappeared around the bend. I thought it was more than a coincidence that we'd met that day. I had never seen her on that trail before, or since. And even though I didn't realize it at the time, a flame had been lit.

I don't know, maybe it was a coincidence. Maybe I was just high from the exercise. But when Shannon showed up at my door, again, I was ready to find out. I had been waiting for Erin to come over, and pick me up to go hit some tennis balls around. I heard someone coming up the steps. It wasn't Erin.

Again, we had to talk about the same old bullshit, and she wanted to know if I'd had a talk with Dane. I told her I did, but so far he wasn't going to agree to her terms, and that she might have to give in a little. She flat out told me that she wouldn't. I just didn't get her. She was begging to get Dane back, but she wouldn't budge from her convictions.

I suggested to her that the both of them were being stubborn. She insisted that she shouldn't have to be the one that gives in.

She said, "If he loved me, he would fight for me."

"Fight who?" I said. "You're not seeing anyone else! It's just you and him!"

I told her to give him some space, see what happens. I reminded her that things have a way of working themselves out. I gave her the set it free speech. You know. He'll come back if it's meant to be. She started to cry. I reached for her, and I began to caress her shoulder.

Shannon leaned into me, and let me hold her in my arms.

She said, "Maybe, I should start seeing other people, and see how he feels about that."

Then she began to really cry. She laid her head on my shoulder, and I could feel her tears running down my neck. I could feel her breasts against my chest, when she breathed. My dick grew hard as a Chinese puzzle.

She lifted her head and looked into my eyes. Her breath intoxicated me. I brushed her hair aside, and kissed her forehead. Again, our eyes met, hers searching. She must have seen the fire burning in mine. The look in her eyes was asking me what I was doing, but a caress of her hand on my cheek, betrayed her. I was about to kiss her on the lips when…

When Erin came bouncing up the steps. Shannon pushed me off of her, like she had awakened from a dream, and found her dog licking her face. I jumped up to let Erin in. I don't think she saw us, but she gave us a weird look. Maybe, she saw something in our faces, I don't know.

I guess only men can be stupid enough to let protective feelings evolve into attraction. Maybe Shannon knew what she was doing, or if she didn't, maybe it was simply the essence of what makes her a woman, that possessed me. Maybe neither one of us had realized what was happening. My only defense was that I was spellbound. I was sure that there must have been witchcraft involved. Who am I kidding? I wanted it to happen, and I believed that she did, too.

Maybe Erin was just put off, because Shannon was delaying our court time. She had been running late as it was. Even so, Shannon managed to draw Erin into the conversation, now enjoying an even bigger audience to cry to.

She took full advantage. She sobbed to Erin that she wasn't dissing her, but she felt that she shouldn't come to her graduation party, cause she didn't want to make it about her and Dane. *Huh? Who'd a thunk that?*

Of course Erin begged her to come. She hadn't fully caught on to Shannon's games, yet.

"You'd better come or I'll be mad," she told her.

Later, Erin told me she was just trying to be nice. Anyway, she and I never made it to the tennis courts. It had started to rain. We went for pizza, instead.

. . . . .

I had begun to bounce back and forth on my thoughts about Shannon.

Does she or doesn't she?

I wondered, "Is she using me to make Dane jealous? Is she merely covering her bases? Or is there really something there?"

Shannon was a mystery. There was so much more to know about her, and I felt like I could go on learning forever.

She had never been the happiest girl I'd known, but it had seemed as though over the past year or so, she had become even more somber and introverted. It had become the norm for her to resemble a woman who was having her period three weeks out of the month.

Even stranger was her attitude towards sex. While she had always worn clothing that accentuated her strong feminine qualities, and still does, she had begun to develop an almost puritanical sense of moral bearing. This is the same girl who had used plenty of sex to win Dane over from Agnes, and had posed for his paradoxical picture gallery.

Even more perplexing was this sudden promiscuous shift in nature towards me. I was sure that it had been more than my imagination that she had been putting the two of us into positions that would be considered compromising to say the least.

It seemed as though Shannon had begun to reveal a second personality that was quickly becoming dominant. She has a side to her that is kind and thoughtful, and wants to please. That side of her, at the time, seemed to be hurting and yearning for affection. But another side of her, one that up to then, she had managed to keep hidden, had begun to overpower her, not to be mean, but to protect.

Shannon did come to the party. She spent most of the time clinging to me. That was because I kept on reassuring her that possibly by the end of the party, she and Dane would be back together.

Dane made it tough.

I prodded him, "Shannon looks great, doesn't she?"

I knew he could see it, and I knew in his heart, or maybe in his pants, that he was willing. I had him on the ropes. I lied, and told him that I believed that she was ready to end her petty bullshit.

Still, it didn't look good. He hadn't talked to her the whole afternoon. I saw Shannon beginning to crumble. I could see it in her face, her body language, I could hear it in her voice. She was crestfallen.

As I was helping Dane load his car, I asked him one more time to give her a chance. I saw his face change, but it wasn't a look that I liked. He shot me a glance that told me that if I didn't shut my mouth, he was gonna do it for me.

They got back together that night. While I sat at home all alone, they went over to Dane's parents' house to spread the news. I didn't find out, until a few days later.

Good for them.

I was glad I was able to help Shannon get what she wanted. The only problem was that by then, I had fallen hopelessly in love with her.

11

"Help me in my weakness," I pled in solemn prayer.

As they led me from the church house, and far away from there.

"My journey's been a hard one, and my time ain't very long. I still don't know exactly, what it is that I've done wrong."

"Much good things have come to you," I heard the judge declare. "You wanted what you couldn't have, for this you must beware. You only cared about yourself, you sinned against your friend. For this you must repent, indeed, and suffer in the end."

The judge went on to end his sermon, and the lesson that he told.

"There's a path that you must follow, don't wait 'till you grow old. If you see your friend has suffered, go and ease him of his pain. And don't mistake what he has lost, to be what's yours to gain."

The moral of the story is, don't let your dog go sniffin' around your neighbor's dog, even if your neighbor's dog has got her ass up, in your backyard.

I was beginning to feel guilty about a lot of things, especially the deal with Ranae. She had mentioned that she was thinking about leaving Miles. To casually fuck another man's wife was one thing, but to break up a family was a whole other sin. For me, seeing her was a purely recreational thing, but she was really into it.

We were sitting on the bench in front of the store when I told her it was over.

"I don't do affairs," I lied.

She threw the book at me. First, she told me that she loved me.

"You're married," I told her.

"And you're a user!" she retaliated.

"You're married!" I repeated, and then I said, "That's so high school."

That's when she reached way down into the muck.

"You made me fall off the wagon!"

I said, "What?!"

She said, "I'm a recovering alcoholic, and you made me start drinking, again!"

"Whoooaaa…! You were drinking way before I ever met you, sweetheart… Your reputation around town is legendary!"

"My reputation?!"

"Yep… And don't play innocent. Almost every disrespectable guy has bragged about getting into your panties!"

She started to cry, of course.

"You made me love you. What am I supposed to do, now… Forget about you?"

"Trust me," I said, "I feel your pain."

I could understand where she was coming from, because Shannon had made me love her, and now I was gonna have to let that feeling die. I was hoping that Ranae would be able to do the same, but around 1:00 in the morning, I heard someone coming up my steps. It was her, and she was drunk.

"Ya gonna let me in, asshole?"

As soon as I opened the door, she went for a hug. I moved away, and offered her a seat. She laughed, and mumbled something under her breath, and then she sat down in the chair across from me. I honestly would have offered her a beer, but she already had one.

"Why didn't you come down to the Hotel?" she asked.

I told her I was tired.

"Tired... You're always tired," she smiled. She got on her hands and knees, and crawled over to me. She started to tug at my pants, and I didn't resist. She slid her hand down inside, and began to caress me, gently at first.

I began to stiffen in her hand, and as I enlarged, she said, "Ohhh, what a big prick you are."

I guess I didn't catch the meaning in her voice, because suddenly, she started to handle me with such force, that it began to hurt. I shoved her away and told her to cut it out. She came at me, again, frantically trying to kiss me.

The whole scene made me feel stupid. There were thousands of guys out that night looking for a piece of ass, and I was turning one down. I dragged her into the bedroom, and started to tug her clothes off of her. Now, she started to fight me.

I smacked her hard in the face, and then I continued to remove her clothes. She hit me back, but I felt nothing. I threw her onto the bed, and forced myself into her. She continued to claw and scratch at me, but after a while, she seemed to grow weak, and instead, she began to hang on.

I started to come, and I could feel Ranae tighten herself around me. She inhaled, as though she couldn't breathe, and I felt her body convulse, as her climax shuddered through her.

Before either one of us had time to recover, I rolled off of the bed and told her to get up.

"Grab your clothes, and get the fuck out!" I said.

"But... Why..." she was still woozy from our fuck, and confused by my request.

I grabbed her by the arm, and pulled her off the bed, and then I started pushing her though the house. I shoved her out onto the porch, and closed the door on her.

She immediately began to pound away, and then suddenly, I saw her face in my window, "Joshua, you give me my clothes, you bastard."

I grabbed her stuff, and when I opened the door, she was there to meet me. She snatched her things out of my hands, and as she did, she slapped me upside the head. I couldn't believe she got me. I shoved her, again, and she fell on her ass.

I could hear her talking to someone down on the sidewalk. It was another woman. Evidently, she had been out there the whole time. I heard the woman tell Ranae that I was an asshole, and that she could do better.

A couple of hours later, as I lay in bed, I heard someone knocking at my door. I ignored it. In the morning I found a note in my mailbox. It said, *I love you.*

· · · · ·

Contrary to what I had said, I felt great about what had happened between Gina and I. Not only had the sex been good, but I felt as though I had gained the upper hand with her. For the first time, Gina had seemed vulnerable to me. A lot changes when you see someone sitting in front of you with their clothes off.

I began to understand, that like her pole dancing at the club, her teasing had actually become a kind of protective measure, a way to take control against everyone and everything that had begun to take advantage of her.

Even so, I decided to do a little teasing myself. I pulled my pants up, and then I grabbed her jeans before she could, and threatened not to give them to her.

"Joshua, come on!" She squealed, "Quit screwin' around!"

I left her sitting bare ass on the table, and I ran out into the store. There was a woman patiently waiting at the deli counter, and I suddenly realized that I had nowhere to go with the stolen pants. I asked the woman to give me a second, and when I turned, Gina met me head on in the doorway of the office.

Thankfully, our collision had knocked her backward, because if it hadn't, our bewildered customer would have gotten more for her money than she had bargained for.

"Hand them over, asshole!" she demanded.

I tossed the jeans to her, and as I returned to the store, she yelled, "See if you ever get in these, again!"

By the time I got out of there the woman was gone.

I did of course. Once I'd gotten a taste of her, I could not get enough. I became tenaciously fervent in my pursuit. And even though she tried to resist me, Gina found herself unable to turn me down. In fact, I found that each time her pants came off, she became more and more insatiable.

Over the next couple days, we couldn't stop fucking. I asked her to move in with me, and surprisingly she agreed, but only on a part time basis. It was a no brainer for her. She'd been hopping from one boyfriend or girlfriend's bed to another for months, and each time, she'd thought she was in love. She figured that I was no different. She knew that I'd keep her for a few weeks, maybe a few months, and then I'd get bored and ask her to leave.

For almost half of her life, Gina had dealt with disappointment. Her biological father was a drug dealer and a loser. He was a hands on, parent, but not in a good way. He had been beating her and raping her, since she was twelve years old. Her mother had divorced him, but Gina believed, that she had left him, not to save her, but because she was jealous.

This revelation disturbed me, but what she told me next, is what really blew my mind. She had been staying with her father off and on over the years since, and during those times, he would get her drunk, feed her pills, and constantly have sex with her.

He would let his male and female friends have their way with her, too. She admitted that on several occasions, she had done it willingly, and eventually, she became pregnant. Whose kid it was, was anybody's guess. Her mother saw her through the abortion.

"He wasn't really a father to me," she explained. "He didn't want to be my father."

When I asked her why she spoke of him in the past tense, she said, "My dad hung himself while I was talking to him on the phone."

That was when the tears finally began to cascade down her face.

Two emotions immediately overwhelmed me. First, I wished her father was still alive, so I could kill him, myself. Secondly, I couldn't help but think that a girl this messed up, would be nothing but problems.

Then, a weird recollection entered my mind. I couldn't help, but compare the similarities between Gina's relationship with her father, to the sordid tale of Temperance and Wilhelm Stone.

The sound of Gina's voice brought me back, and it calmed me.

"Well... I guess you're gonna dump me now, huh?"

I knew that whatever came out of my mouth next, could not be something that would hurt her. I'd had no problem being mean to Ranae, and I felt bad about that, but Gina was on the bubble. I knew for once, someone had to be on her side.

"Ain't gonna happen," I replied assuringly. "You and me, we're thick as peanut butter. You're stuck with me."

I know it's supposed to be as thick as thieves, but I like peanut butter.

·   ·   ·   ·   ·

Now, people think Stormy is flaky and dumb, but that's just a persona that she assumes on Thursday and Saturday nights, when she's working the bar at the Hotel. She wears skirts that are so short, they barely cover the admission to the amusement park she's got between her legs. Trust me, it works. Most men hang out there just to watch the show. She makes a killing in tips.

Her dumb act is also used as a defense strategy. When I first met her, and naturally started to hit on her, she confided to me that she'd been abducted by aliens. That worked, too.

This chick's out there.

And suddenly, the two and a half feet of counter space that separated us, felt reassuring.

Later, on a slow night, the real Stormy Samuels and I got to know each other. Not only did we have a good laugh about the alien story, but I discovered that she is smart, and that she'd read a lot of interesting books, which of course, I then had to read. She was involved in different kinds of charity work. She could sing, and she was learning to play the guitar. She was into exercise, so we started to run together on the trail. And of course, one thing led to another.

Things were looking swell in Stormyville, who was into open relationships and didn't give a shit how many other women I saw, as long as I didn't get all possessive on her. I was most certainly content to adhere to that logic. All I had to do now, was pray that Gina could, too.

Being the typical self-centered, red blooded, American horndog that I am, I believed that I would be able to handle the revolving door of women that had begun to grow around me. For the time being, I decided not to tell Gina about Stormy. I wasn't ready to lose her, and I knew the thing with Stormy would pass.

It was the news that Ranae brought me that almost sunk the ship. She had come into the store for her daily cup of coffee and a box of feminine napkins.

When I made a crack about a visit from her monthly friend, she said, "Oh that's right, I won't be needing these for nine months."

"Wait a minute," I stuttered, "you tryin' to tell me something?"

"Only if you're asking."

"No…"

"Yes…"

"But…"

"Oh, don't worry, asshole… The kid's not yours."

12

Any other guy would have assessed the situation and cut his losses. I tried, but Shannon wouldn't let me. Within a few weeks, she and Dane were right back to where they had left off, and Shannon came right back to me with her problems.

I knew that Dane had just about had it with all of my meddling, but I took a chance, and I decided to tell him that Shannon was fishing, again. I didn't tell him about the other stuff, not wanting to bum him out, or perhaps, because I did not want to feel his fist pushing my nose through the back of my head. I promised to back off.

He said, "Don't worry about it, Bro. I know how Shannon is."

I vowed to myself that I would spend less time with the two of them. But it seemed like after that, Dane went out of his way to make sure that the three of us wound up together, as much as possible. The two of them were playing some kind of game. I wasn't sure if it was with each other, or with me, but as usual, found myself stuck in the middle.

Dane called me, and asked me to pick Shannon up, and head on down to Gettysburg. He wanted to introduce us to his new hippie friends, Clayton Bogart and Brigid Young. It was gonna be a fun weekend for all of us. During the drive, Shannon was already worried.

"I don't know about these hippies," she sniveled. "They probably smoke pot. I'm not sure I like this at all."

I just shook my head.

This is gonna be fun. She's sulking already, and we're not even there, yet. I can't wait.

We arrived with plenty of time left in the day, and the weather was beautiful, so the three of us went for a walk around town. Dane told us that we wouldn't see Clayton and Brigid, until the next day, to Shannon's temporary relief.

We decided to take one of the nightly ghost tours Gettysburg had to offer, designed to both provide historical enlightenment, and to also empty tourists' pockets of their money. We picked the Jennie Wade House, because she had been the only civilian to succumb to her wounds, during the three day Civil War battle, that had taken place there.

I paid for the tickets in advance, and we headed back to the house. Believe it or not, Dane and Shannon had already started to bicker and fight in the couple of hours that we'd been there. I found myself wishing that Gina had come. It had already become apparent that our deal was on shaky ground, as well. She had just become too drawn to the seedy world she'd grown accustomed to.

I tried to keep the two of them happy. I was starving, so I figured we all just needed something to eat. I bought some steaks and a pumpkin pie. As always, Dane was the chef. Shannon made the salad. I was hoping that the camaraderie of preparing a good meal, would bring our spirits up.

But what should have been fun, was quickly going down the drain. Dane was looking forward to the tour whereas I guess Shannon wasn't. She was sulking, and Dane was sulking, because she was sulking. We managed to eat, and then we took turns in the shower. Me, then Shannon, then Dane.

While Dane was in the shower, Shannon came down from upstairs. She grabbed Dane's laptop and sat right next to me on the couch, and started to browse through the Jennie Wade info.

The girl was wearing nothing, but panties and an oversize t-shirt, which she had purposely cut low, to reveal plenty of delicious cleavage. She began to snuggle up against me, and crossed her legs, so her knee was resting on my thigh. Trust me, I didn't mind this at all, but then my mind drifted to the sound of the shower, and I snapped back to reality.

I got up and moved to the chair, and after a few minutes, Shannon set the laptop on the floor between us, and stretched out on the couch. Feigning disinterest in me she reached down and played with the laptop for another minute, and then she propped herself up, and when she did that, her t-shirt hung down so openly, that it gave me a clear shot of both of her breasts, nipples and all.

And she knew I could see them, because I was staring right at them, and she did not move, until she heard the shower shut off, and then she ran upstairs, and waited for Dane to come up, as though she'd been there the whole time.

And if she had really been holding out on him the past couple months, she was obviously under a lot of pressure herself, because when Dane got upstairs, she let him have it, and she made sure I heard her letting him have it, and for the next forty minutes, I heard laughing, moaning, the bed creaking, the floor thumping, and the two of them chasing each other around the room, and it was getting late, and I started to yell up there for them to hurry. After things had quieted down, of course, and when Dane came downstairs, he was happy as a clam.

We barely made it on time for the tour, because Dane insisted that we walk, me twenty paces ahead of them, the two of them hugging and giggling the whole way.

The tour itself was interesting. I had stayed behind in a bedroom, as the others continued with the tour, and left alone, I began to feel the presence of another in the room with me. Suddenly, a chain that had been placed around the bed as a barrier, jerked and began to sway, as if someone had passed by it.

In the next moment, I watched in amazement, as an indentation in full human form began to appear on the mattress. It took a minute, but once I had gathered myself enough to be able to speak, I thanked Jennie Wade for her company, and then I left her to join the rest of the tour.

Dane and Shannon had a great time during the tour, and afterward, when we stopped for a beer. But as we continued our walk back to the house, one thing was said, and then another thing was said, and then they began to yell at each other, and then it all fell apart, again.

· · · · ·

We spent the next afternoon browsing through a huge flea market, that stretched up the four streets that met the town square. It was another gorgeous day, each of us finding an item or two that we'd been looking for. The WWII Army field jacket that I acquired, was enough to make my weekend, alone. We topped lunch off with some ice cream, and then it was back to the house to regroup for the evening.

Around 8:00, Clayton finally showed up, having to extend Brigid's apologies for not accompanying him. We sat around for a while, listening to music, and as expected, Clayton turned Dane and I on to some good weed. Shannon went into her shell, barely speaking a word. That is until we decided to go ghost hunting. Then all she did was complain.

We followed the railroad tracks directly behind Dane's house, down to an old train station, where we found a few out of service passenger cars.

Inside one of the cars, Dane pretended to be a conductor asking, "Tickets, please," of his unseen commuters.

We had nothing with us to record any evidence, our investigation this night being purely for fun. But as usual, I sensed the presence of someone else in one of the cars with us, and as we were leaving, I'm certain that I saw someone lean out of a doorway to watch our departure.

As we were climbing up over the hill towards one of the battlefields, Shannon suddenly turned and slammed Dane with such force, that she almost sent the two of them back down the embankment.

"I saw a man standing down on the tracks, about a hundred feet that way," she whined, pointing south of where we were standing.

"Could have been a security guard?" I asked.

"I don't know," she sniffled, almost in tears. "It was the full figure of a man, but I swear I could see right through him!"

"Maybe we should check it out," Dane suggested.

"It could be security," I repeated. "I say we keep moving."

Clayton said nothing, but he was shaking like a leaf and his eyes looked as though they were ready to pop out of their sockets.

"Let's just go home," Shannon quivered, clearly spooked by what she thought she had seen, and not at all comfortable with the situation in general.

Dane said, "C'mon."

He continued to lead us down the path, almost dragging Shannon behind him. Shannon, in protest, freed herself from Dane's grip, and began to hang all over me. Dane didn't seem to care, one way or another, and despite being wary of what Dane might be thinking, I didn't mind it at all.

When the path seemed to come to an end, Dane became unsure of where we were at. We stopped for a minute, and when we did, Shannon backed herself into me, and that's when Sluggo started to get scared, because this hot chick was now smothering him with her hot ass.

Dane told us to wait where we were, while he and Clayton went to look for the clearing. Shannon had begun to notice Sluggo's growing discomfort with the situation, and once we were alone, she quickly turned around, and began to relieve him of his tension. Sluggo, who was not a very smooth young fellow, began to slobber all over her hand.

Neither Sluggo nor I could understand why Shannon had suddenly felt such compassion for our needs, but we were glad she did. The one time that she looked up at me, her mischievous smile told me that she'd been wanting to do it for a long time, the look in her eyes searching for approval.

Maybe, she was just paying me back for leaving me hanging at the house those couple of times. Little did she know, she had left me holding Sluggo more than a few times, since I'd known her.

Anyway, when Dane finally returned, she went straight back to hanging on him, but it was towards me that she started to direct her bitchiness. Maybe, she was pissed, because I hadn't returned the favor back there on the path, but that's how quickly her mood had begun to swing.

She started to complain that if we get busted, she'd get passed on for the job she recently applied for. Of course, even though Dane was right there, she was telling all of this to me, as if I'd become her traveling therapist and whipping boy. What did she want me to do? Dane was the one who had led us there.

We crossed the field, and took cover under a bush, everyone suddenly afraid to venture out into the open. It was really dark, which limited our ability to see anything clearly, that was more than forty feet away.

I left the others at the bush, and made my way to a monument up by the road. This move did not sit well with Shannon. I could hear her making comments about my mental capacity with words like, idiot and moron. She was probably wondering if maybe she had succeeded in emptying my brains, along with my testicles, a few moments before.

Suddenly, a cop car came flying up the road, out of nowhere. I rolled behind the monument as he passed by, unsure if he saw me. I thought I was tripping. This guy spins the car around, like in the movies, and pulls up slowly in front of the monument. Now, I began to think for sure that he had seen me.

He turned off his lights, and cut the engine, but he never got out of the car. He just sat there for a few minutes. Emboldened by their cover, I could hear Dane telling me to stay put, and then him and Clayton laughing.

Then I could hear Shannon telling them to, "Shut the fuck up!"

After what seemed like forever, the cop started his car and zoomed off. I waited another minute, and then I crawled over to the bush, where I found Dane and Clayton laughing their asses off, and that's when Shannon began to call me even more names, like stupid bastard and asshole.

When we thought the cop was gone, we took off running across the field to the tree line, and all of a sudden we saw Clayton flying through the air, hit the ground and do a roll, and spring back into full stride without missing a beat.

Once we got to the railroad tracks, Shannon started on me, again. And again, why me? She didn't have a thing to say to Dane or Clayton. I tried to explain to her, that the security cop wouldn't have done anything to us, except tell us to leave.

As it was, I had begun to suspect that he had done that whole car spinning, lights out performance, just to scare us, and add to the thrill of the night.

13

We weren't playing for the crowd. We never do. Instead, we form a circle, facing each other, feeding off of each other. Even the drummer pays little attention to what is going on in the rest of the room.

The place was filled with people. Some playing beer pong or foosball. Most standing around talking and getting high. Some watched the band. The band never noticed.

This was the usual scene during the Friday night jam sessions at Tubby Hatfield's barn. Tubby's real name is Glenn. As a kid Tubby was huge. Hence, the nickname. As he grew older and taller, he kind of evened out. These days, he weighs in at a slender three hundred pounds.

But he's a great guitar player, just as most of the other musicians in attendance were good at what they did. The core of the players were members of Dane's band, Maelstrom. These days, their gigs had been few and far between, but the guys were always ready to play when Dane would call.

Dane showed up late. He'd come home for the weekend, and of course, he had to stop at Shannon's house first. And as what had become the norm, she did not show up with him. He was not in a great mood. He would never let it show to the others, but I could see it. His visit with Shannon had not gone well.

At first, he didn't even want to play. I simply pestered him, until he was ready to crown me with whatever was in reach. Dane wasn't drinking. He never drinks if he has to drive. By the time he did finally step in to play, the main band had pretty much finished for the night, and most of the players now were drunk. He hung in for a couple of tunes, but the inconsistent playing of the other guys quickly began to frustrate him, and they never even noticed when he put down his guitar and walked away.

. . . . .

The next day, we decided to do an overnighter. When I use the term, I'm referring to our overnight camping excursions, held anywhere on the two hundred some acres that make up the Bruckner's yard. This time, Shannon decided to grace us with her presence.

I've always been impressed with the fact that she will always do almost anything that Dane asks her to do. Things most girls wouldn't want to be involved in, like riding dirt bikes, kayaking, hunting, and fishing. When I say most girls, I'm not including country girls, some of whom have bigger trucks than the guys. I simply have never seen Shannon in a pair of cowboy boots.

More than anything, it's plain to see that it's just not her style. I know that her true interests lie far from the world that she has reluctantly allowed herself to be drawn into, in order to be with Dane.

I just don't understand why she would rather try to get him to bend to her will, when she could simply go out and find someone who actually shares in her interests. Is she in love with him? Or is it that she simply feels that it's better to remain in a situation that she is not totally happy with, just because it's safe?

Anyway, for me, none of that really mattered, because as long as she remained in Dane's world, she would remain in mine. On the overnighter, she had come reluctantly, because Dane had asked her to, but it was easy to see that she would have rather been somewhere else.

We piled seven people onto two quad runners, and one utility vehicle, and made our way to the site. Dane always picked the spot, and though we had our favorites, he would always try to find a new one. Of course, we always had to take the long way to make it more interesting, and if the floorboards of the vehicles weren't submerged in water at some point, he wasn't a happy camper.

By evening, the camp was set. Dane and Shannon shared a tent, I had my own, my cousin Brent Collins and his girlfriend, Bethany Simpson in another, and the Cooder brothers, Philo and Sam in theirs.

The Cooder brothers were Dane's closest friends next to me and Brent, and like me and Brent, they were members of Dane's band, Maelstrom. Like Dane, they were easy going, and always up for anything. The two of them put up a street sign at the head of the camp that said, *Motley Manor.*

We really roughed it for supper, with steaks, hot dogs, chicken filets, potato salad, and corn on the cob. As the darkness of night began to surround us, we were thoroughly stuffed and ready for a couple of beers, and a few ghost stories.

The Cooder brothers love story time, and one of their favorites is my tale of the legend of the Allegheny Woodbooger. Of course Woodbooger is our name for our local sasquatch.

As the story goes, some large animal had been ransacking barns and chicken coops, presumably helping himself to a quick meal. It got to where some women were afraid to go out at night, because the Woodbooger was known to throw rocks at people, and even peep into a window, now and then.

Brent's grandma Maddie Holcomb claimed that the Woodbooger had been outside her house, which was basically a cabin in the middle of nowhere, several times, and that one night, she had seen him, "Plain as day, in the moonlight, as he walked past my kitchen door."

"Several others can also attest to seeing a hairy man like creature, that walks on two legs, and smells like a wet dog that has rolled around in a pile of horse shit," I drawled, as my story came to an end. "Keep them nostrils clear boys," I said, looking directly at Sam and Philo, "cause if you smell something' funky, it might be the Woodbooger comin' right for ya!"

Sam shivered, and his eyes began to dart around a hundred miles an hour.

Suddenly Brent farted and said, "Here he comes now!"

The laughter broke the spell, and everyone grabbed another beer.

The girls were afraid to venture off into the darkness to pee, so they squatted next to one of the tents, after making the rest of us promise not to look.

Once everyone had settled back down, Brent said, "Let's hear the one about Winefred Stover."

Dane said, "You tell it, Brent."

Brent looked at Bethany and said, "Go ahead, Dane... You tell it better."

"Well, alright then," Dane began, affecting a deep woods accent. "Ya all better hang on to yer chair, cause this'n might be 'nough to curl yer pubes... If ya got any."

As he said this, he looked directly at Bethany, who instinctively closed her legs, and nervously circled the audience with her eyes.

"All right Dane," Shannon intervened, trying to look disgusted for Bethany's sake. "Just tell your stupid story, already!"

Dane threw her a knowing smirk, and continued.

"They say that back in the time of the pilgrims, a girl name Winefred Stover once lived on the hill, right above where we're camped this night.

"They say that on the day of her wedding, not an hour after they'd given their vows, she found her husband, screwing her cousin against the side of the barn, where their reception was being held. Of course, she kept her promise and stayed with her man, but she never let him consummate their union."

Shannon was now beginning to fidget in her seat, a sigh of displeasure escaping her lips. She too, had begun to search the faces of her fellow listeners, for a glimpse of what they might be thinking.

"Because of this," Dane went on, "Winefred's husband began to enter into one affair after another, until he'd bedded nearly every single woman in town. It was when he started an affair with a married woman, that he met his demise. The woman's pissed off husband walked in on them in the middle of doin' it, one night, and shot them both, just as they were ready to come.

"The husband then turned the gun on himself, and that left poor Winefred alone and humiliated, and the subject of rumors, told in a whisper by every woman in church on Sunday, and rounds of laughter from every man in the pub at night.

"They say that Winefred began to spend her nights laying in bed, masturbating, until she had come so many times, she started to go mad. She began to sit under a tree by a cliffside, and finger herself silly, and it was said that you could smell the scent of her pussy all the way into town.

"Finally, one night after she'd fucked herself to the brink of death, she jumped off the cliff in shame, and also to stop herself from ever touching her pussy, again. But some say she was cursed, because of her unchaste affliction, and her spirit masturbates under that tree by the cliff to this day.

"They say that on just the right night, and if the wind blows in just the right direction, you can catch the scent of Winefred Stover's pussy juice, clear down here in this hollow where we sit, right now."

Everybody knew it was just a funny story, but just the same, each guy among us sat in silence after the laughter had died down, and imagined what it would be like to get a whiff of Winefred's rose bush.

Shannon didn't think it was funny at all, and at bedtime, when Dane decided to sleep out under the stars on his hammock, she went to their tent, even more insulted.

There was no way for the others to know, but it hadn't slipped by me that part of that story was directed towards Shannon, and I'm sure by her reaction that she had gotten it, as well.

About an hour after everyone had bedded down for the evening, Shannon crawled into my tent and snuggled up close to me. My dick immediately hardened, but I knew it wasn't the time. What I also knew was that on this night, a shift had begun to take place. It was this night that Shannon made me realize that it was no longer just her and Dane. It was this night that I learned that she had become willing to make it three.

At some point that night, someone looked in on us. As they turned away, I saw that it was Dane. I couldn't put my finger on it, but I just got the feeling that Dane knew he would find us together in my tent, that night. Almost as if he had planned it that way.

. . . . .

For all outward appearances, Shannon would remain Dane's girlfriend. Nobody had even said anything, but between the three of us, it just became an unspoken pact. Dane and I had been sharing Shannon already for months, in different ways, but for the same reason. It happened gradually, naturally. To us, it seemed normal.

Shannon loves Dane. Dane loves Shannon. I love Dane. Dane loves me. I love Shannon, and Shannon... Well... She loves Dane. But I was growing on her. Dane and I were becoming the only two people on earth that Shannon felt safe with. The only time she felt at peace was when it was just we three, alone, together.

But Dane continued to have other interests, and that continued to frustrate Shannon. I knew she had begun to sleep with him, again, because she told me she had. The idea had been that he had been seeking the comfort of other women, because she was holding out on him.

"Now what is his reason?" she asked me.

The problem was not, that I didn't know the answer. The problem was, that she asked me this question, as she was stroking me into an erection, and since I wasn't planning on coming into her hand this time, my mind was directed towards the part of her anatomy that I did plan on coming into.

Of course, as I began to enter that part of her anatomy, she continued to interrupt my thought process.

"Use a condom," she nagged.

"I don't have one."

"You never have one… You're playing with fire, you know."

"I'll take my chances."

"Sooner or later, you're gonna get me pregnant."

"I wouldn't mind pregnant sex."

"You men are all alike."

"Where have I heard that before?"

"Oohhh. That's… starting to feel good."

"I'll bet you say that to all the guys."

"You're bad."

"I love you."

"Liar."

"If you have my kid, you'll have to marry me."

"So that's your plan."

"Yep."

"I'll say that it's Dane's."

"You'll have to fuck him first."

"Silly… I've been screwing him, since that night in Gettysburg, when we went to see Jenny Wade… Ooohh, that is really starting to feel good."

"I figured that. Just wishful thinking. I want you all to myself."

"Joshua, can I ask you something?"

"Yeah, what?"

"Do you ever fuck without talking?"

.   .   .   .   .

That was a legitimate question. I do tend to talk during sex. I don't know why. Maybe I do it to keep myself from coming too fast. Or maybe I just like to let my partner know I'm enjoying her company. Maybe subconsciously, I do want to get Shannon pregnant, too. Anyway, she's the one that started the conversation. Women, see how they twist things around?

Things were getting twisted around. To answer Shannon's question, Dane was fucking other women, because he was seriously trying to leave her, only I couldn't tell her that. Not when I was a half an inch from her pussy.

And now, I was beginning to feel guilty about having sex with Gina, and Stormy. I felt like I was cheating on Shannon. I let myself fall ass deep in love with her, and now I was wrapping myself around her finger.

Well, I didn't have to worry about Stormy. I had been spreading myself pretty thin, and not paying very much attention to her, which was insane, because she really is every young guy's wet dream. There never was any kind of a relationship, anyway, and she really didn't miss me. In the meantime, she had started a fairly solid thing with Will Buckley, aka Big Red, the owner of Big Red's Harley Shop.

At the same time, Gina had pretty much quit staying at my place. She was sinking fast. It didn't take much on my part to figure out that she and Heather had begun a relationship, and were also shooting heroin, together. I couldn't help, but think that this pretty young girl was gonna wind up like the women that lived upstairs at the Hotel. If she lived long enough.

I considerd these thoughts and others, as I sat in my living room, watching it rain, as I so often did when I needed to think. I was interrupted by the noise of my phone ringing, only to be surprised by Stormy's voice when I answered.

"I was just thinking about you," I lied.

"Good because I need you, right now!"

"Well, come on up," I laughed, "I think I can help you."

"Wrong, Lothario! I need you to come down here, and scrape your neighbor off the floor. He's out of his skull!"

"Right," I told her, "I'll be there in a minute."

I wasn't looking forward to this.

About a month and a half before, Otis had caused a huge scene in the main intersection of town. The cops found him ranting and raving at every car that passed by. He was immediately given a ride to the county psych ward, where he spent about fifteen days. Then they gave him a room at some detox center for a month.

The landlord couldn't throw him out, because of a clause in our lease that states that a tenant can't be evicted for any reason due to illness.

The time away didn't help him much, though. This was the day he had been released from the clinic. When I got to the Hotel, I found Otis sprawled on the floor, stoned drunk, and mumbling something about being fucked in the ass by a horse.

"That, my friend," I explained to him, "was more than I needed to know."

. . . . .

I called Dane and told him that I felt kind of weird about the whole Shannon thing. He told me there was no reason to start feeling that way. He said that everything was as it should be.

"Everyone expected me and Shannon to get married and stuff," he explained. "We had fun for a while, Bro, but it's done run its course. The best thing for you to do is to dig it for what it is, and in the meantime, you need to get down here and ride that Harley."

When I arrived in Gettysburg, Dane had another surprise for me. He had bought a real nice bike from a guy whose brand new wife, didn't like motorcycles. It was a two tone blue and white 1994 Harley Davidson Heritage Soft Tail, with twelve inch handle bars, and lots of chrome. It was equipped with a 1340 CC V twin motor, studded seat and saddlebags, and white wall fatty tires.

"The guy was moving to Florida," he laughed, "and his wife said the bike wasn't goin'. That Bro, is why me and Shannon are history. No woman will ever tell me I can't have my toys. Pussy is pussy, and sometimes, it gets old on ya, and ya get tired of ridin' it. I'll never get tired of ridin' this lady."

He had a point, but since my thing with Shannon was just beginning, it was hard for me to see it that way. I should have though. I'd known Shannon for a long time. I knew how she was. I saw what she put Dane through. Why would I think it would be any different for me?

The difference between me and Dane is, that nobody makes him do anything he doesn't want to do, and I love pussy more than motorcycles. I hate to admit it, but a woman can get me to do almost anything for the sake of her vagina.

Anyway, Dane had a plan to do a lot of riding for the next couple of days, and part of the plan involved corrupting me into having sex with Dawn Marie Swanson. And because of the fact that a woman can get me to do anything for a taste of her snatch, no one saw this as a problem.

I've always wanted to be with Dawn Marie. Even though they are identical twins, Dawn Marie's lusty attitude has always made her look hotter than Gabrielle.

Dane and I wasted no time in heading down to their house in Maryland. Evidently, this was a route Dane had been taking on a regular basis. He had given up the pretenses, and had been seeing Gabrielle, regularly. Apparently, this had left Dawn Marie feeling a little lonely, and it was also apparent when we got there, that she had been expecting me.

It had been a long time, since I'd had a girl pay so much attention to me. They made us dinner, made sure that our beers were never empty, and basically treated us like kings. The Swanson sisters sure knew how to treat their men right.

Just before bedtime, Dane looked over to me and winked. I nodded back at him to let him know that I finally saw what it was that attracted him to these girls. They were the exact opposite of Shannon, who was needy and insecure. These girls expected nothing from their man, except a little attention in the sack at night.

Far from the wild animal that I thought she would be, Dawn Marie tenderly saw to my needs in bed. I don't think that I'll ever be with a more beautiful creature than she was that night. It was only when she was certain that I had been completely sated in every imaginable way, that she let herself succumb to her own inevitable pleasure.

For that night anyway, I had forgotten all about Shannon, and had fallen in love with Dawn Marie. This lovely soul had made me realize that I had been coveting something that was not meant to be.

But it would take a lot more than just one night of enlightenment, before I was going to be willing to give up what I'd been wanting for so long.

Dane knew the deal, and he was willing to wait as long as it took to say, "I told you so."

. . . . .

The problem was that Dane couldn't, or wouldn't, tell Shannon that he was done. And if he couldn't put her down, how could I? She wasn't just anybody. She was one of us. We were like three kids, who had used our favorite pocketknife to make a blood oath. It just couldn't be that easy.

For me it was a no brainer. I had always loved Shannon. We've always been friends. She'd only recently allowed me to fall in love with her in the way that lovers do. She'd only just invited me to experience the physical realm of her being.

Why was I out tomcatting around when I'd finally been given everything I'd always dreamed of? The answer to that was easy. She was not in love with me, Shannon loved Dane, and I knew deep down that just as Dane had been my gateway to her, I had now become the connection that held her to him.

She had developed a mild interest in me to be true, but it was merely a collateral interest, the result of her misguided belief that it was what Dane wanted. She was willing to have sex with me just to keep the man that she loved, and in the meantime, she hoped that he would become jealous enough to end the charade.

Maybe Dane was using me too. Maybe he was just using me to keep Shannon occupied while he tested the waters. As much as he kept saying that he was through with her, it didn't seem as though he was in much of a hurry to make it official. Shannon was never my girlfriend. She was Dane's.

Even if he was just keeping her around, until he found someone else, it wasn't fair to her. Those other girls might have been taking care of him in bed, but Shannon was the one who cleaned his house, kept his life in order, and was always there when he needed her. She was the one who comforted him when he was down. The other girls weren't the ones who thought of him on his birthday and at Christmas.

. . . . .

Shannon had recently landed a good job as a result of a business course, she had been taking, and in a short period of time, had received a promotion. To celebrate, she used part of her savings to buy a new car, which she then impulsively drove to Gettysburg to show Dane.

When she arrived, she found Dane in bed with Gabrielle, and immediately turned around and drove straight to my place. She looked as though she'd been crying for hours. I had just been about to take a walk over to the Hotel, so I invited her to join me. She was up for it.

Once we'd ordered, she started. I didn't know that the name Gabrielle was synonymous with words like bitch, slut, and whore, but apparently it is so. She had a few choice words for Dane, too, like asshole, cunt lapper, and swizzle dick.

Then she turned on me.

"And you!" she sniffled. "You told me to fuck him! You said, he'd like it. You said, he'd be happy. You said, he'd stop cheating! Well, I fucked him… A lotta good that did me. You were wrong, buster!"

At least she only called me buster. I felt bad for her. I knew this was gonna happen. I was wrong. I thought maybe Dane would be true to her, if she slept with him. That is, until I realized that she had been too late with the happy meal. Dane had already tried another item on the menu, and he found out that he likes the taste of it, better.

"I never promised he'd quit cheating," I countered.

"I might have insinuated…"

"Don't get cheeky, fucker!"

Okay, I'd talked myself from buster, down to fucker. The conversation was sinking.

Think quick, now. It's not too late to move back up to buster.

"You gonna buy me another beer, asshole?"

Oops, too late.

I tried, in the gentlest way possible, to explain to her that maybe their relationship had run its course.

I said, "Maybe you should think about letting him go. The two of you had something good, while it lasted. Try to remember that, and don't try to beat it into the ground."

"Beat it into the ground, Joshua… Really?!"

At least she was calling me by my name, now, but her diatribe went on and on. It had seemed as if she hadn't heard me at all. Why was I even there? She sure as hell wasn't. She was off in another world, somewhere, and she was getting drunk, fast.

So was I, and hell, after a while, I just wanted to fuck her. I had this beautiful, hot, sexy, drunk girl, who I was totally in love with, right in front of me. Her boyfriend was halfway across the state, fucking someone else, and she knew it. I saw a revenge fuck in the making.

I had to get her back to my place. I told her that she was too drunk to drive, and I was too drunk to drive her home. I told her that her parents thought that she was in Gettysburg, and she could stay at my place. She didn't argue.

Shannon doesn't drink much, but when we got to my apartment, she wanted to finish herself off. I let her have another beer, and as I looked at her, I saw the same look of pleasurable indifference that she displayed in the last few photographs in Dane's picture gallery.

I still hadn't forgotten those pictures, and I'd been dreaming of the chance to get some of my own. It was brilliant. I'd get her to slowly undress, and then I'd have her, and I'd have the pictures too. I was ready to spend the next hour begging, but surprisingly, she agreed.

She was wearing a black long sleeved, turtleneck minidress, which I told her she could leave on for a moment. I asked her to climb onto my bed, and remove her panties. She reached under her dress, and slid them up over her knees, and down to her ankles.

"Leave them there," I said, and then I told her to prop her hands behind her back, and keep her knees raised in front of her, so I could just see the dark dusky spot between her legs.

Though she was cooperating, I knew I had to move fast. She was plastered, and still not in a good mood. My luck could change at any moment. The look on her face was already evolving into aggravation, and drunk as she was, I could detect a little humiliation. I began to focus the camera, and center the shot.

"Come on Joshua... I have to pee!" she sniveled.

"Lookin' good, sweetheart," I assured her.

I snapped the shot, and as I began to prepare for another one, Shannon puked all over herself. One click, one shot, it was over. Automatically I felt bad for her. I tried to help her out of her dress, but she shoved me away, and went into the bathroom, where she emptied the rest of the contents of her stomach, into the toilet.

As she peed, I began to wipe her face, and she began to tug at my pants. Within seconds, I went from feeling sorry for her to wanting to lick the pee off of her pussy, and I got on my knees and began to do it. She began to beg me to fuck her. I could see that she was barely holding on.

I had managed to get my pants down to my ankles, when she shoved me onto the bed. She climbed on top of me, and began to grind herself against me. She stopped just long enough to let me enter her, and then she slid down the length of my shaft, so slowly that I thought I would come before her ass hit my thighs.

She was so wet that her juice began to run down into the crack of my ass. I wondered how a chick that drunk could get that wet. I immediately wanted to have a taste, but the girl wasn't budging, and she let me know why.

"Fuck me, Joshua! Fuck… Me! Pretend that I'm Gabrielle! Pretend that I'm whoever you want me to be! Get me pregnant, if that's what you want, but promise that you only want to get me pregnant, Joshua! Promise you'll only ever fuck me!"

I promised, because at the time, I meant it, and when I came into her, it felt just like it had the night I got Sara pregnant. After I'd begun to come back down to earth, I thought, *Oh, boy… What if…?*

Shannon was passed out on my chest. The protective feelings had begun to return, so I helped her out of her dress, put one of my t-shirts on her, and tucked her into bed. I took her dress down to the laundry room, and as I waited for it, I watched her sleep. When I finally climbed into bed, she snuggled up against me, and she didn't let go, until the morning light had awakened her.

. . . . .

Shannon was kind of mad at me in the morning, but not for anything in particular. She had no recollection of my taking her picture. She had no idea what we'd talked about exactly. She was sure that I'd taken advantage of her somehow, though. I filled in the blanks a little, with my own version of the evening's events.

She wasn't in any hurry to leave, or to get dressed.

"Oh, so I made you get drunk," she laughed. "And then I had my way with you. Ya know, in the mood I was in last night, I almost believe you."

We shared a few more laughs over a cup of coffee, and then she climbed onto my lap, and made love with me on the very same couch, where only months before, she had sat without a clue of how I had really felt about her. It struck me how she could give herself to me so freely, now, and I knew that unlike the night before, she would remember that I'd told her that I loved her.

The mood didn't last long. Shannon took a shower, and by the time she'd gotten dressed, Dane had showed up. I'd had visions of the two of us spending the day together, but when she left with Dane, I was reminded of my place in the pecking order.

I had become Dane's back up, his cover guy for when he needed to keep Shannon under control. I had become Shannon's go to guy, when she couldn't have Dane. Only a few moments before, I had begun to believe that Shannon was falling in love with me. Dane's arrival had brought me back to reality. She had used me, just the same as I had used her.

I've become convinced that even when we love someone, we're still using them for something. Everybody uses each other for something, even if the thing we're using them for is love.

14

Dane had completed the audio course that he'd been taking, so he decided to stick around town for a few days. After he'd had a heart to heart with Shannon, he stopped back at my place to fill me in. He told me that he had one final project to do on Saturday, in which he needed my participation. I told him that I would be happy to help, but I was waiting to hear the real lowdown, and I didn't even try to hide it.

"What about Shannon?" I asked him.

"Shannon's fine," he replied. "As a matter of fact, we're going shopping later, and she's gonna buy me that acoustic bass, I been wanting."

"Dude that thing ain't cheap… How much is it?"

"About twelve hundred bucks."

I told him that it was cool, but that it was a lot of money for her to spend on him. I told him that he had better think about letting her do that, if he didn't plan on staying with her.

I kidded him and said, "That's a bigger commitment than a piece of ass."

He said, "I know, I better think about it." Then he said, "What's the difference... Everyone's mad at me, anyway."

"Who's mad at you?" I asked.

"Everyone," he replied. "Shannon's mad at me, because I'm interested in Gabrielle. Gabrielle is mad at me, because I'm concerned about Shannon. My mother is mad at me, cause she thinks I'm doing Shannon dirty."

"Your mother's not mad at you," I said.

"She insists that Shannon and I belong together."

"Well, Shannon is a good Irish girl."

"She says we should be married."

"She just wants to see you happy."

"I won't be happy with Shannon. She's not who you think she is."

"What's that supposed to mean?"

"I'll tell ya some time. Right now I gotta go."

"That's it... Leave me hangin'."

"I'll tell ya about it over the weekend."

"I'll hold ya to it," I told him. Then I said, "Listen Bro... You do what you gotta do. You're not obligated to please anybody but yourself. But I will say that you should decide what you want to do... For Shannon's sake, at least."

"And for yours, too?" he asked, and then he left me to answer that question myself.

"Yes, Dane... For mine, too."

. . . . .

On Saturday, Dane hosted an outdoor show at the Cornwell Inn, in Fairfield, Pennsylvania, a small town about twenty miles southwest of Gettysburg. The inn has been around since the 1700's, and is said to be very haunted.

It's a quaint little place with a definite historic feel about it. The original building still exists, but had been expanded in the 1800's. It consists of eight rooms, a tavern and a fine dining area. The owner of the inn happened to be a guy named Val, who also owned the studio where Dane attended school.

The event was part of the town's yearly Apple Festival. It was a gorgeous September day. The show was a joint project of Dane's and a fellow student's, to finish their training. In reality, it was just something that Dane, his classmate, and Val had cooked up for some fun. More than just an instructor, Val had collaborated with Dane on other projects, as well.

Dane had brought Shannon back to Gettysburg with him, so I knew there was no chance of us having that conversation he'd promised. He'd also brought the bass guitar that she had bought him, which meant that he was not going to be cutting her loose, any time soon.

I barely made it on time, but Dane was in a good mood.

"I hope you brought your guitar, brother," he smiled.

"You know it," I assured him, as I unpacked my gear.

Dane and I played first, and then the rest of the bands followed. The music was mostly laid back acoustic stuff, ranging from bluegrass, to folk, and finally a hippie jam band called Black Juju, which we all took turns sitting in with at the end.

Shannon was her usual self, sitting behind the soundboard, and frowning most of the time. Clayton and Brigid were there. They tried to break the ice with Shannon, but she ignored them. When I say ignored, I mean, ignored. They were standing right in front of her, talking to her, and she would not even acknowledge their presence.

She especially ignored Brigid for the simple fact that she's female. On the other hand, within moments of meeting her, Brigid had captivated my interest, completely. This detail did not go unnoticed by Shannon, who decided that there was no time better, for she and I to take a walk around the fair.

During our stroll Shannon began to lighten up a little. The both of us enjoyed the classic car show, and the craft booths that lined the street. We had a cup of coffee, and I bought her a caramel apple. She bought a couple of knick-knacks that had caught her eye, and for a while, anyway, she seemed content. Once we'd returned to the site, though, she immediately slipped back into her sullen mood.

I couldn't keep my eyes off of Brigid. She was beautiful, part Native American, of Cherokee descent. She told me that she had a little Persian blood in her, too. Her aura was contagiously peaceful, and the way her eyes twinkled when she smiled, just floored me.

Shannon was not happy. She had found herself in the complicated position of having to be jealous of two guys. You would think that she would be secure in the knowledge that between Dane and I, only one of us could possibly be with Brigid, unless of course, she pictured the two of us tag teaming her.

She had no reason to worry about Dane, he wasn't interested, and she had nothing to fret about with me, either. I'm not so much of a jerk that I would humiliate Clayton by hitting on his girlfriend in his presence.

The day turned out to be a complete success for Dane and his friends. Afterward, Val invited us to spend the night at the inn, on the house. He was even gracious enough to include Clayton and Brigid.

At dinner, he confided to Dane that their class had been his last. Running the inn had become a full time passion, so he was retiring from the studio. Though bittersweet, the tearful revelation had left Dane feeling honored. He told Val that what he'd learned from him was invaluable, and that he'd grown to consider him a good friend. Val assured Dane that he shared the sentiment.

Dane and I hoped to do a little ghost hunting, but since the inn was filled with other patrons, it was just not possible. Val did let us go down into the basement for a while, which was a spooky place. Once again, we had nothing with which to record any evidence. I did, however sense that we had company with us, and when I let it be known to the others, the girls decided that they'd had enough.

At bedtime, I shared a room with Clayton and Brigid. I offered to sleep on the floor, but they insisted we share the bed. Since none of us had any sleepwear we stripped down to boxers and panties, respectively, Brigid choosing to go topless, as well.

"I usually sleep in the nude," she confided.

At some point in the night, I woke up to find myself snuggled up close to Brigid, who was now completely naked, my hand resting securely on her breast. Immediately, a neurosexual blast of energy began to telegraph its way from my brain down to my crotch, but Brigid's soft steady breathing told me that she was fast asleep, so I figured that I'd better not awaken her. At least not this night.

On the drive home the next evening, Shannon barely spoke a word to me. I tried to carry on a one sided conversation, but eventually I gave up. Even our relationship, strange as it was, had begun to take on the characteristics of a tired union. We had begun to resemble a couple who had become bored and disappointed with each other.

As I spoke, I could see that I was only succeeding in annoying her, and at one point I said, "You just really want to smack me, don't you?"

The comment had managed to draw a slight smile on her face, but the look in her eyes told me that my assumption had been correct. Despite her mood, Shannon could not completely hide the fact that she cared for me. When she broke her silence, and offered to spring for something to eat, I immediately took her up on it. Afterward, she took over the wheel, and ordered me to get some rest. As I dozed off, I began to feel content that the kind-hearted girl, that I couldn't help but love, was still there with me.

. . . . .

A few days later, Gina paid me a visit. I couldn't help but notice how pale and emaciated she had become. She was really drunk, and probably stoned. When she kissed me, I could smell a woman's sex all over her face.

"Where are you coming from?" I inquired.

"I was with Heather," she admitted. "We had an argument, so I left."

"Must have been a fun argument," I responded. "I just got a taste of her snatch... Tell her it tastes great next time you see her."

"I won't be seeing her, again," she sniffled. "I broke up with her."

I didn't care at the moment. Heather's scent had quickly put me in the mood, and even a pale and thin version of Gina, was enough to do it for me. I slid my hand up her thigh, and she responded by slipping hers down my shorts.

I jumped a little, and she said, "Cold hands, warm pussy."

"It'll never happen, again," she promised, as she slid down the length of my shaft.

I was so turned on, that I came, before she had time to get warmed up, and I came hard.

"Wow!!!" she marveled. "The Johnstown flood!"

I'm not sure what it was that had gotten me so fired up, but I made sure that Gina's needs were met... Three more times. I can't even remember at what point it was that we both passed out. All I can say is, that for a stoned chick, she had a lot of energy.

The next afternoon was when the situation began to get a little weird. Gina had gone out. Where to, I didn't know, because I never asked her where she was going. I didn't want to know. I'd decided to take a nap on the couch, and had barely begun to drift off, when I heard a knock at the door.

I was surprised to find that it was Gina's mother. I asked her to come in, and sit down.

"Gina's gone out," I explained, then laughing I added, "and it could be for days!"

"That's why I'm here," she confided. "Can we talk?"

"Sure... Uhh, Mom?"

"Call me, Dana."

"Yeah... Dana... Would you like something?"

"Tea... Please... Chamomile."

"Right up," I said. As I prepared the tea, Dana talked.

"I'm worried about Gina," she admitted. "I may have to take her away from here. I've left her step dad and I'm moving to New York. I want to take her with me, to get her away from this scene. Oh, not you, mind you, just away from that club, and those junkies."

As she spoke, I began to fantasize about screwing her. I couldn't help myself. She was gorgeous. She looked so much like Gina, only with shorter hair. She had the same glistening green eyes as her daughter.

Get a hold of yourself.

When I returned with her tea, I sat down on the couch, next to her. She didn't waste any time moving closer.

"Wow, I really like your jeans," she cooed, grazing her fingers against my thigh.

She commented on how well they fit, and then she slid her hand up my leg, until it pressed against my crotch.

I knew what was about to happen. I knew it was wrong, but I couldn't stop it. I had no will. It was as though I was under a spell. I knew the woman was into some strange stuff. Gina told me that her mom was into the occult. It suddenly occurred to me that she must be a witch. A very beautiful witch.

Not long after Dana had left, Gina returned. She had bought some steaks, and was in an unusually happy mood. I felt like a jerk. I felt compelled to tell her what had just happened with her mother. I knew I shouldn't. I just couldn't stop myself. I just blurted it out.

"I slept with your mother."

"I know."

"How?"

"She told me that she wanted to seduce you… and I told her to go for it."

"Why?"

"I knew it would happen, eventually. She's been wanting to get me back for my father."

"So… What… She told you about it?"

"Nope… I watched."

"What?!!"

I had thought I'd heard it all, but this was beyond bizarre.

"You looked in through the window? Where were you? What did you do?"

"I got turned on... I fingered myself... What do you want to hear? Do you think that I enjoyed watching you lick my mother's pussy?!"

"How long were you there?"

"I didn't stick around for the fireworks, if that's what you're wondering."

"Well, I still don't understand why you did this. You encouraged it. You let it happen. You set the whole thing up. You could have stopped it. And your mother... I don't know about her....!"

"So you're saying that I'm fucked up?"

"No... It's just not normal."

"Then, I'm fucked up."

"No... Look... I'm sorry for what I did."

"You better be."

"I am."

"No you're not."

"Yes, I am... I'm sorry. I'm begging you to forgive me."

Gina thought for a minute.

I could see the wheels turning in her head, "Well..." she said, "at least you had the decency to admit it."

At this point, I had no idea what I was admitting to. This girl had just turned me upside down, and inside out. I didn't know whether to feel fortunate or wary. What I did know, was that after we ate those steaks, I planned on making Gina get drunk with me, and then I was gonna let her turn me upside down and inside out the fun way.

As had become usual of late, Gina didn't stick around. She left quietly in the morning, before I had awoken. Despite our petty jealousies, we had basically become friends with benefits, evolving into a pattern of being there for each other, during our down times.

From the moment I'd met her, I had realized that she was a very unstable person. It was better that nothing serious had ever developed between us.

. . . . .

Even though he'd finished school, Dane decided to honor the lease on his house, and stick around Gettysburg for a while. He likes it there, and at one point, he considered living there. After all, his thing with Gabrielle had become a full time deal.

Time had passed into October, and fall in Pennsylvania had begun to set in. That meant cooler temperatures, morning frosts, and the leaves changing colors before they withered, and fell to the ground. It also meant that it was the season for pumpkin patches and haunted trails.

Dane called me, and asked me to pick up Shannon, and meet him at the farm that Saturday. He was bringing Clayton and Brigid with him for the weekend, promising to show them how the people in the western half of the state rolled.

After one of Mrs. Bruckner's famous country breakfasts, the five of us piled into Mr. Bruckner's Chevy Suburban, and drove north to McConnels Mills for some hiking and rock climbing.

It turned out to be a perfect day, as we toured the mill, and then wound up out at Hell's Hollow, which boasts a really nice waterfall. Of course, Shannon was wary of Clayton and Brigid, who took regular breaks to maintain their buzz.

At the mill, Dane and I politely declined their peace offerings, partially to placate Shannon. For myself, I like to enjoy the outdoors with a clear head, and I knew that we'd have plenty of time to relax, once we had settled down at Dane's camp in Pymatuning.

The camp consisted of a double wide trailer, and a huge shed, filled with canoes, kayaks, four wheeled vehicles, fishing gear, and just about anything else you could possibly need to have fun in the wilderness.

We built a nice fire and commenced to cooking supper, after which, Dane and I serenaded the others with a little pickin' and grinnin'. Once the pot came out, Shannon excused herself, and went inside. It was then that we all began to tell our stories and get to know each other better. The story I liked the most, was when Brigid told me that she and Clayton were simply friends.

After a while, it began to rain, so we decided to move inside, and watch a movie. Shannon sat away from the rest of us, alone in the kitchen, sulking and frowning the whole time. She had treated Clayton and Brigid like shit, the entire day, barely speaking a word to them. Finally, she just got up and went to bed. Of course, Dane felt obligated to accompany her, so he sheepishly bid the rest of us good night.

Clayton and Brigid felt bad, and they wondered why Shannon had acted that way. You'd have thought that they would have been used to it, from the last time they'd been with her. But the fact is, most normal people can never get used to horrible, unwarranted behavior like the kind that Shannon had dished out to them.

Clayton later told me, that they felt like they had hung out with me, more than with Dane, which was true, and a shame, because they were nice people, and Shannon would have liked them, if she'd given them a chance.

Clayton's observation was correct, but just how spot on, he couldn't have anticipated. Brigid and I had gotten along, especially well. Our breezy conversation had become more personal, as the night wore on, the two of us moving closer with every word.

She had sat modestly apart from me during the movie, but by bedtime, she had caught my vibe, and was eager to return it. When I winked at her, as we said goodnight, she caught that, too, and about an hour later, it did not surprise me when she came tip-toeing into my room.

15

He begins his quest at her peaking tips. Then down southern valleys, to her nether lips. She quivers and squirms and she sighs like a girl. As he grazes his fingers, over her dewy pearl. She feels kinda funny, her belly does flutter. A river soon flows, with her honey butter. To her dusky flower, the passage lies narrow. For it's swollen petals, he aims his hot arrow. He teases her some, as she clutches her pillow. Then he fills up her nest, with his weeping willow. To a warm rippling wave, their senses will heed. That comes from the loins of two lovers in need.

Lately, I hadn't been able to get Brigid off of my mind. I missed the sound of her voice, and those Persian brown eyes. I missed the scent of her. I also could not forget our clandestine carnal dalliance, that night at the camp. As I lay in bed at night I longed to see her again.

Of course, the first place I stopped upon my arrival in Gettysburg was Dane's, where I wasted no time in expressing my interest in seeing Brigid. Dane was pleased to accommodate me, and he immediately began to try to contact Clayton to set up a get together, later that evening.

Secondary to my desire to see Brigid, was my interest in viewing Dane's photo gallery, once more. At this point I was pretty sure that he wouldn't mind. So I asked him to fix me up. He got me to where I needed to be, and then he excused himself to call Gabrielle.

"Don't get any on my equipment," he laughed, as he left me, almost sure of my intentions.

I was especially hoping to find the pictures of Shannon that he'd shown me before, but instead, I stumbled upon a new batch. I was stunned. In these, Shannon was with one of the Swanson sisters. The pictures showed the two girls completely naked, and in the process of having sex, tongues lashing at one another, fingers penetrating glistening genitals.

In one photo, Dawn Marie, whom I had identified by her fury patch, had spread Shannon's vagina wide open, the camera illustrating the dark abyss, just beyond her opening. The feeling of the shot, both frightening and profound, in that it displayed the infinity of our existence, the unknown, the primal chaos before creation.

The photos ended with the girls' faces in each other's muffs, but the picture that struck me the most, was the third one, which showed Dawn Marie, sitting on a couch, Shannon kneeling in front of her, facing the camera, Dawn Marie's hands massaging Shannon's breasts, the look on Shannon's face, clearly that of a girl, who had begun to let herself succumb to the pleasures that only moments before, she had so virtuously resisted.

I was just about to signal Sluggo into the batter's box, when I heard Dane enter the room behind me.

"The pictures were taken when we were still in high school Bro. When Shannon and Dawn Marie were still friends. When they were still lovers."

Dane had scared the shit out of me.

"Dude, what the fuck is going on here?" I stammered.

Not only did he scare me, but now he was telling me things that made me wonder if I even knew him at all, or Shannon, for that matter.

I asked him what kind of game the two of them were playing. Shannon, with her Polly Purebred routine, was obviously not the chaste and proper innocent that she'd like everyone to think she was. And why was she constantly trying to titillate me with her wiles?

"Just doin' you a favor, Bro. You've always wanted her... Well, have her... and have all the bullshit that comes with her."

"What is the problem with her?" I asked him. "There are obviously two different Shannons."

"Ask her yourself, Bro. She'll tell ya... if ya ask her. All I can tell ya, is that the girl is damaged."

"If she's so fucked up, why don't you leave her?"

"Can't man... Wish I could... But I can't. She won't let me. She won't let you, now, either. She's a witch, Bro... A fucked up witch... Really. Once you've sunk your dick into that pussy of hers, you'll remain under her spell, until she's ready to let you go."

"This is a joke, right...? You're putting me on. I mean, I believe in witchcraft, but Shannon? C'mon, dude... I know she's been acting strange lately, but she's a prude. How can she be a witch? She's just not that deceptive. Confused, maybe, but not a witch."

"Something happened to her, Joshua. Something, someone else caused to happen. Someone let evil into her... And she doesn't even know it. She's been promised, Bro. Someone made the deal. A daughter to... I can't even say it. Just ask her, Bro... She'll tell ya."

Dane had called me by my name. That's how I knew that he was serious. But in my mind, serious didn't mean that he was right. The way I had taken it, he had been insinuating that Shannon had been involved in some kind of ritual, and had been offered to the devil, himself.

I believe that evil sprits do exist, but the devil, the selling of souls, I've never had it hit home like that. Dane hadn't told me everything. He'd held back a crucial piece of information. Who was the someone, that he'd repeatedly referred to? I was going to have to get that part from Shannon. The problem being, how do you get a girl to admit that somewhere in the near future, she might possibly become Satan's flavor of the month?

.   .   .   .   .

While the revelation of Shannon's impending promotion from evil seductress to queen of the damned, weighed on the back of my mind, I still had my evening with Brigid to look forward to.

Dane and I drove to Gabrielle's, and then the three of us met Clayton and Brigid at the Cornwell Inn, where the five of us spent the evening chasing the spirits that were being offered from behind the bar.

I'm not sure if I still had Shannon on my mind, or if I had just been a little nervous about Brigid, but I was pretty well drunk by the time we'd left the inn, and had driven to a spooky covered bridge to hang out, and smoke a joint.

Supposedly, the pot had been treated with opium, and I guess I had too much of that, too, because by then, I was thoroughly wrecked, and my night with Brigid was quickly going down the drain.

I still can't remember the exact sequence of events during the next hour or so, but I had obviously fallen asleep, because by the time I'd awakened, the others were gone, and it was just me and Brigid, alone at her house.

I had been dreaming that Shannon had become a succubus, and was in bed with me, snacking on my tasty treat. Just as she was about to get to the cream filled center, and suck the life out of me, I woke up to find Sluggo in Brigid's hand, and Brigid gently attempting to revive him.

Coming from unconsciousness, my first reaction was to push her off of me, but Sluggo was clear headed enough to tell me that it felt really good, and that I should let her continue. At first, Sluggo seemed a little shy, but as she continued to pet him, he warmed up to her, fast, and began to wag his tail.

What happened during the next hour or so, is easy for me to explain, because from the moment she had climbed on top of me, to the precise moment when the both of us had climaxed for the third time, I had fallen completely in love with her.

Now, I admit that I fall for almost any woman that is nice to me, especially once we've made love. I also find that I'm able to love more than one woman at a time. Maybe, I don't even know what love is. It is possible that sometimes, I mistake infatuation for love, but I do know that the warm feeling that I was now experiencing for Brigid, had come more from my heart than my loins.

So much so, that during the drive back to Dane's house the next morning, Brigid and I began to make plans for me to move to Gettysburg.

.   .   .   .   .

So, I'll keep the memory, that for her I could fall, cause it's better than never having loved her at all.

I saw the ghost, again, and the more I saw her, the more she was beginning to look like Brigid. It had been a few days, since I had left Brigid with our plans, and had returned back home, and something just didn't seem right. She wasn't answering my calls, and neither was Dane.

The night before, I'd had a dream that I was driving down a winding road, that I'd never been on before, and as I rounded a bend, I saw a girl slumped over the guide rail. She was only partially clothed, wearing a sweater, but nothing from the waist down.

I stopped my car, and went over to her. Hesitant at first, I summoned the courage to lift her head, and discovered that it was Shannon. She was dead, maybe, by only minutes.

I immediately became creeped out, and I suddenly began to feel as though I was being watched. I spun around thinking that she could have been murdered, and that her killer might still be near. I saw no one. We were alone there. Not even a car had come by.

I turned to Shannon, and that's when I finally let my grief overwhelm me. I looked around, again, and then I knelt down before her, wrapping my arms around her thighs, and resting my head against her buttocks. Memories of her smile, her voice, began to enter my thoughts, and then sadness.

I began to imagine a tear running down her face, and realized that it was my own, and when I raised my head to brush it away, I was pleased to discover that she had begun to lubricate. I was pleased, because that meant that I had mistaken her passing, and that she was still alive.

I called out her name, but she didn't answer me. I shook her, but she didn't move.

She must be alive. She's still warm, soft, wet, her honey running down her leg.

I pressed my face into her crotch. I began to lick the juice from her thigh, but it didn't taste like it should. I realized that her body had simply begun to release fluids. I became ravenous. I lowered my pants, and I pushed myself into her.

As I continued to ravage her, it felt as though her skin had begun to cool to my touch, though it could have been the breeze that had begun to swirl around us. On the inside she had begun to feel hotter and hotter, almost unbearable heat, and within minutes I came, hard.

Within seconds of my orgasm, I once again became consumed with sadness, and also now, guilt. Shannon's body, also within seconds, had begun to decompose. I pulled her up from the railing, and held her, tight in my arms. I kissed her hair, her face, her lips, and when I moved her away to look at her, she was no longer Shannon. She was Brigid.

The next afternoon, Dane finally called.

"I don't know how to tell you this, Bro," he said, but I already knew.

He told me that Brigid had driven her car over an embankment on a winding road near her house. The shoulder of the road had slid away, about a month before, and had been under reconstruction. There had been no guide rail to stop her. He said she'd been there about a day and a half, before the road crew came back to work there, and found her.

He said that it was normal that even Clayton found it difficult to get a hold of her, sometimes, so no one had reason to think anything out of the ordinary.

But almost immediately thoughts had begun to form in my mind.

Why, during almost every moment that I'd spent with Brigid, had visions of Shannon consumed me? Did Shannon, in fact possess some sort of supernatural ability to cause events that could affect people's lives, around her? Was she somehow able to hold me to my promise that I'd only love her?

It did seem as though my relationship with Brigid had somehow been interfered with. But no, it had to be a coincidence. It had to be fate. Brigid's death had been an unfortunate accident, and nothing more, and my thoughts of Shannon had been nothing more than feelings of guilt that anyone would experience when breaking a promise to someone that they supposedly loved.

16

I like how if you let your vision blur a little, it looks like a fur tree, where her bush meets her bum crack.

I was sitting at my kitchen table looking at the picture that I had taken of Shannon a while back, and that's what I was thinking. I was also thinking that I might have to do something about the erection that this vision of carnal exquisiteness had bestowed upon me.

I know that it could possibly fall into the more than we needed to know area, when I convey the details of my friends with benefits relationship with Sluggo. You might also find it weird that I feel the need to masturbate to a photo of a girl who is willing to fuck me.

But damn it, sometimes things can get a little weird when you're desperate, and these were certainly desperate times. My new girlfriend had just died. Shannon was being difficult as of late, and Gina, who was about to leave town, had been having her period, all week.

As bleak as things had been, Gina had given me reason for hope. She had promised me that when her period was over, she would come to work hot to trot, and that she would be wearing a skirt to signal the occasion.

Well, she finally did come into the store wearing a skirt, but she was twenty minutes late. Our boss, Eugene was freaking, because he had somewhere to go, and he tore into her. They got into a huge pissing match, and that's when Gina told Eugene that she was done.

She went outside and left Eugene gagging for air, he'd already had one heart attack.

"Stop her," he choked.

I raced out, after her, and I begged her not to quit.

"What will I do without you?!" I pleaded.

"You've got a hand... Use it!" she screamed, and then she told me that she was leaving for New York with her mother. "Sorry, Joshua," she sniveled, "but I can't take one more second in this bum fucked town!"

I cried, as I watched her walk down the sidewalk to the Hotel, where her mother was waiting to pick her up.

After work, I went straight to the Hotel, and ten Guinnesses later, I still hadn't forgot about that skirt. Camouflage, and I was sure at that point, that she had been going commando, underneath.

Even Stormy, who always wears a skirt, couldn't take my mind off of it. After she'd closed up, she came over to the house, and sat on my face, but I was down for the count, and she left, disappointed.

So, it was not good, the condition that I found myself in the next morning. With the taste of Stormy's nest still on my lips, and a picture of Shannon, who is the vision of all my wet dreams, and Sluggo, who was begging to be taken for a walk, and a left hand, who wasn't doing much of anything, at the moment, what else could I do?

And Shannon, maybe she was using witchcraft to sabotage my extraterritorial activities. It was beginning to make me wonder.

There's something mighty peculiar about that Morrison girl, she gets mad at me, and then all of a sudden, I can't hook up with anybody.

Or maybe, it was the work of a much higher power that was trying to teach me a lesson. I'd thought that the best way to get over Brigid, was to dive tongue first into another woman. I'd never even taken the time to grieve the loss of the beautiful person that I had been falling for.

Despite these things that I had begun to ponder, I still had a minor crisis to resolve, and as I had begun to do so, I was suddenly made aware that apparently, the forces at hand were sometimes quick to change their mind, because just as Sluggo had begun to break into a full gallop, and was about to start foaming at the mouth, my phone rang.

And of course, I answered it, and the voice on the other end said, "I need fucked."

.   .   .   .   .

Pregnant sex is the most erotic form of love making to me. Especially if the kid inside your partner's belly is yours. During Sara's short time with child, making love to her had made me realize the essence of manhood, the feeling of virility, the masculine spirit, the power of procreation.

Even though Sara had not been given the chance to show physical signs of pregnancy, there was most certainly a glow about her, the essence of her womanhood. Making love to her during those weeks, she had never seemed more beautiful to me.

Sex with Ranae had felt the same way for some reason. The difference being that she was about five months pregnant, and had been well on her way to showing it. Her breasts had filled out some, and her belly had started to swell, as the living being within her had begun to grow.

Where normally I had found her to be a moderately pretty girl, she now looked absolutely beautiful to me. The sex was incredible, for me, at least. Her vulva had begun to swell along with everything else, and the feeling of a fat pussy wrapped around my cock was nothing short of heavenly.

For Ranae it was a little different. She had begun to lubricate less, and she was finding it harder to achieve orgasm. Still she enjoyed it for what it was to her, being that she had been sated with the intimacy of bonding with the guy, who's child was in her belly.

Yes, after the first of the several times we made love that night, she admitted to me that it was my kid. I was happy, of course. So happy that I wore her out, three more times.

"This can't hurt the kid?" I asked, after the second time.

"It's a boy," she laughed, "in case you were wondering… And no it can't."

This was Ranae's key to holding on to me. I couldn't even be sure that she was telling the truth. She'd been carrying the kid for five months, letting me think it was Miles'. I'd had a feeling all along, though. Since, the first time she'd told me that she was pregnant.

My only other question was, "Where do we go from here?"

17

A couple of weeks before Christmas, Dane decided to move back home. His love life had taken a turn, like mine had. Gabrielle had suddenly turned cold towards him, apparently not happy that he wouldn't make the effort to break clean from Shannon.

He decided to keep the place in Gettysburg, though, in case he needed to get away, or in case Gabrielle got lonely some cold winter night. But he moved most of his stuff back into the house he'd bought from his dad. This made Shannon happy, though this time it was clear that it was Dane's house, and his alone.

At this point, everyone could see that their relationship had run its course. They spent most of their time together, fighting, and Dane had begun to pick on Shannon, more than ever.

When I say he picked on her, it wasn't just with words. It had become a physical thing. Poking her, and wrestling with her, tangling her up and holding her down. He thought that he was playing, at least that's what it looked like to me, but Shannon didn't like it.

Yeah, a little horseplay can be fun between two lovers, as long as its private and consensual, but the guy isn't supposed to wind up on top. He's supposed to let the girl win. I tried to remind Dane of that, but he didn't listen. And Shannon would never really fight back. She would just submit to him, and then become humiliated.

But most of their real fights were the result of Shannon's desire to get Dane to settle down into her dream of domestic tranquility, and Dane, who is usually pretty laid back, would eventually grow weary of her excessive concern for inconsequential details, such as minding his money and cleaning his house, and then he would get pissed.

I've said it before, and I'll say it say it again. There is nothing wrong with the life Shannon wanted for the two of them, but Dane just wasn't ready for it, and he wasn't going to be, for a long time to come.

I, on the other hand, would have been perfectly willing to settle into that kind of life with her. I liked the same things as Dane, but not to the same extent. Dane planned on making a career involving music. For me, it was just for fun. Sure, almost every guy dreams of being a big rock star, but I just don't possess the talent, where Dane truly does.

When the two of us play together, it's Dane that the people come to see. Sure, he brings out the best in me, and we do harmonize beautifully, and I do enjoy every second of it, but I know that Dane carries me, and that he's meant for bigger and better things.

Now, don't get me wrong. I still wanted to be somebody. I still wanted to accomplish something. But I had dreams of being a writer, and I knew that I could still do that. Writing was my dream, Shannon my muse. I knew that I could be, famed novelist Joshua Harrison, and still be Mr. Shannon Morrison, at the same time.

Anyway, Shannon wasn't interested in living her dream with me. Dane was the center of her world, and somehow, she was going to keep him there. She was determined, even if it meant enduring a lot of disappointment along the way.

. . . . .

Dane called me one evening, and invited me over to help him and Shannon trim their Christmas tree. Within minutes of my arrival, it became apparent that their demeanor would be no different than that of any other occasion, as of late.

Shannon didn't like the way he was stringing the lights on the tree. He thought it was fine. Dane wanted to order pizza. She started to lecture him about spending too much money. He changed the channel on the television.

She said, "Hey I was watching that!"

I have to admit that this sounds like every couple on the planet. Shannon's complaints were legit. Dane was doing a shitty job of trimming the tree. Yes, they should watch their money. He should have asked, before changing the channel.

But Dane liked the way he'd been stringing the lights. He sincerely thought he was doing a good job, and it was really his tree, anyway. Shannon had expected what should have simply been a fun project to be a work of perfection.

Plus, Dane had changed the channel, because we had planned on watching a few Christmas shows that were about to start, and as far as I could tell, Shannon hadn't been paying any attention to the television, until Dane picked up the remote.

I guess it's true that it takes two to tango, but my point is that this just went on all of the time. This night was supposed to be fun, and what was really wrong with pizza? I would have probably paid for it, anyway.

I just got up, and left.

Dane said, "Where are you going?!"

I said, "You're both driving me nuts, and I'm going home to watch Charlie Brown, in peace!"

About a half an hour after I got back to my place, Ranae showed up at my door, with a bowl of popcorn for the two of us to share, and a six-pack of Guinness for me. We snuggled on the couch, and we watched *Charlie Brown* and by the time we'd gotten about half way through *It's A Wonderful Life* she had that fat pregnant pussy wrapped around me so tight, that it gave a whole new perspective to the phrase, "peace on earth."

She'd also made me forget about Dane and Shannon, at least until she decided to tell me about her bullshit ultimatum. Ranae had known about most of my extraterritorial dalliances with other women. She had known about Gina, and Stormy, and especially about Shannon. Up until this night, she had said nary a word about it.

Now, out of the blue, she was telling me to cut it all out. That she preferred that I see her exclusively, as if I was betrothed to her. I laughed in her face. There was no way that was gonna happen, pregnant or not. And even though Miles knew that she was upstairs fucking me, and didn't seem to mind, she was still married to him.

I knew that Miles had to know that the kid wasn't his. I was almost sure that they didn't have sex. I assumed that he figured it was mine, but hell, I still didn't know whose kid it was. When I demanded that she show me the proof that I was the daddy, she got really pissed, and went back downstairs in a huff.

. . . . .

The next time I saw Dane, which was a couple of days later, he and Shannon had broken up, again.

She had decided that they needed to, "Take some time."

Perfect, right at Christmas. But it didn't matter, because this was the beginning of the strange era of the two of them being officially "broke up," but still seeing each other all of the time.

The only thing that would be different was that she cut Dane off from sex, again. And since, when she broke up with Dane, she broke up with me, too, that meant that this time, I was banned from getting into her panties, as well. The irony in that it turned out to be that Shannon had unwittingly done for Ranae, what I had refused to do, only days before.

What was even weirder, was that Shannon had begun to date some guy named Peter, that worked with her, that no one ever saw. She had given Dane the green light to sow his oats, and she promised that she would do the same. While Dane took her idea to heart, and immediately began to pursue other women, I would venture to guess that the Peter that she'd been seeing had merely been the handle of her hairbrush.

Shannon also went back to her practice of leaning on me for information. She constantly tried to get me to slip up, and give her some kind of detail about what Dane was doing, or who he might be seeing.

She told me that her reason for breaking up with him, again, was because, one night, he had left her house saying that he was tired, and was going home to get some sleep. She said that he'd been doing that a lot, lately, so she looked on his phone, and saw that he'd been calling Kelly Lynne, those nights. So, this night, she'd followed him home, and spied on him, and saw that Kelly Lynne was there. I told her that it was just her imagination, and that Dane and Kelly Lynne were just friends.

I told Dane what Shannon had done, and he admitted that he did have Kelly Lynne over, but that he'd left Shannon's house, because, "She was having her period, was in a bad mood, and had fallen asleep."

He swore to me that he and Kelly Lynne did nothing that night, but watch television.

I did notice that Kelly Lynne had begun visiting Dane, a lot more often, after Shannon broke up with him, again. Eventually, one night, I had arrived at his place just as she was leaving. She had a particular glow about her, I'd say post-coital in nature.

Dane asked me to come into his studio, and listen to something. What I heard, was one of the most beautiful voices ever. It was Kelly Lynne. They had recorded several duets together, Dane, naturally providing all of the instrumentation. It sounded amazing.

"So, this is what you two have been up to," I laughed.

Dane offered me a couple of tokes from a doobie, and once the glow from the grass had settled in, I began to remember the glow on Kelly Lynne's face. I made the comment that I thought that she was talented, and that I'd also gotten the impression that she liked him more than just friends.

To that, he finally admitted that, "Sure, we're friends. We can talk to each other about stuff... And yeah... We take care of each other, every now and then, too... If ya know what I mean."

. . . . .

Remarkably, this was also the period when, out of no-where, Agnes walked back into Dane's life. Even more re-markable was the path she took to get there.

I was sitting at the bar, pouring my woes out to Stormy, when someone sat down beside me, wrapped her arms around me, and placed a kiss on my cheek.

"Sorry, I'm late babe. It's that old car of mine. I almost couldn't get it started."

Then to Stormy, she said, "I'll have a Bailey's on ice, love... When ya get a minute."

Stormy frowned at the interruption, and then turned to fetch the drink. Before I'd even turned, I knew who it was. It was the voice, that raspy drawl. It was Agnes.

"Fancy meetin' you here," she laughed.

That laugh. That hearty, happy laugh. It seemed so long ago. It was coming back to me. I asked her how she'd been doing, and she told me that she'd been going to school for nursing, and that she was working at the local Max and Erma's, to earn her keep.

"How about you?" she asked.

I told her that I was working at the convenience store a-cross the street, and then I joked that I was gonna write a novel about it, titled, *Confessions Of A Convenience Store Clerk.* There was that hearty laugh, again. Is it possible to fall in love with someone in five minutes?

After a little more small talk and another beer, I began to feel compelled to apologize for Sara's, and my own behavior that night at the party.

Agnes smiled.

"I was pretty loaded that night," she said, "but I knew what I was doing. I went to that party lookin' for it. I would have fucked any decent guy there. When I saw you, I knew we were gonna do it. I just wasn't countin' on Sara. I didn't even know she was like that. I figured her for a cold fish."

"Sara's cold, alright," I assured her, "but not in the sack."

"Well not to dis' you, but I enjoyed Sara so much, that it helped me make up my mind about my friend Ally."

"Oh, don't tell me… You're a lesbian, now."

"No… Me and Ally are both straight, but she was buggin' me for the longest time to try it, and I kept resisting. After Sara, I had the courage to let Ally seduce me one night in her bedroom. Imagine, two high school girls… Her parents were in the living room watchin' television. I was so noisy, Ally had to cover my mouth, so they wouldn't hear."

I was beginning to imagine, and so was Sluggo.

"So, it was just that one time?"

"No we did it a few times, off and on. But hey, I'm the kinda girl that needs a big strong man in my life… And yeah… A big hard cock in my pussy."

Okay, at this point in the conversation, the seam in the crotch of my pants was about to give. I knew where this was going. I just couldn't believe that Agnes could forgive and forget that easy. What's more, I couldn't believe that Agnes had turned into a bad girl.

We went over to my place, and it was there that she told me we were going to fuck, but only under one condition.

"I want you to fix me up with Dane."

Huh?!!!

I had begun to think that I had died and gone to heaven. I had thought that all of my woman troubles were over. I had become sure that Shannon's pussy had no power over me, as Dane had warned. And now this.

Really?!

"I want him back," she continued, slowly, as if the thought of what she was saying had pained her. "Now that that little twat is out of the picture."

"But…"

"Do you want laid, right now?"

"I… Of course… of course, I do." Now I was stuttering.

"Then, promise to fix me up with Dane."

My, how news travels, fast. I couldn't even fathom how she knew that Dane and Shannon had split, but at the moment, I was in no position to argue, especially, since Sluggo was beginning to get impatient with me.

"Yeah… Okay… Whatever the lady wants."

"Good," she cooed.

As Agnes began to take her clothes off, I pretty much just stood there like a dope, and watched her. The only way to describe her properly, is to say that she is a very healthy looking girl, with blond hair between her legs to match the hair on her head.

I was in love with her, before we even touched. Sluggo, on the other hand, had begun to drool, and I began to fear that he might not have the restraint to wait for me and Agnes to get started.

To calm him down I half jokingly asked her, "Will there be anything else, my lady?"

To which she replied, "Yes… Now, I would like you to stuff your cock in here."

She inserted a finger into her, now glistening split, and then licked the juice from it. Then she did it, again, and this time, she put it in my mouth.

"Finger too small," she sniffled, "need cock."

Well, I gave her my cock, but first I gave her my tongue, and a couple of my fingers, and she liked it fine. As a matter of fact, she liked it so much that she asked me to do it, again. But when I woke up in the morning, Agnes was gone. The only proof I had that it wasn't just a dream was a note on my nightstand that read, *You promised.*

18

All Agnes would have to do was simply show up at Dane's house, or anywhere that he was at, to be with him. I'm sure that modesty had kept her from doing something that would make her seem too eager. She certainly didn't have to seduce me, but I was glad that she did. I hoped that she had intended to sleep with me at some point, regardless of the timing.

From the moment that I showed up at Dane's door with Agnes, it was like high school, again. When their eyes met, the two of them became transfixed. I could see it in both of them. Dane was completely mesmerized. The brazen, self-assured girl that I'd been with only a few nights before was gone.

Within moments, it was as if I wasn't even there. With nary a word between the two of them, Dane took Agnes' hand, and led her straight into his bedroom, closing the door behind them. I went out the back door, closing it behind me.

I was glad for the two of them, but I was also tired of playing second fiddle. It seemed like all of the girls wanted Dane, and they all used me to, either get him, or keep him. Gabrielle Swanson was the only one that had never approached me for help, but I put that down to her being so completely shy, that she would never dare.

How Dane ever got Gabrielle to pose for those lusty pictures, I'll never know, but one thing I did know, was that once, again, I needed to stay out of that part of his life. And once, again, the only problem was that, neither Dane nor his girl-friends, would let me.

As soon as Shannon found out that Dane and Agnes were back together, again, she was all over me. Only this time, she really planned on making Dane jealous. While up to this point, there had been an agreed upon effort, by the three of us to keep my affairs with Shannon from the public eye, Shannon, now had decided that her and I had become an item.

If it weren't for the fact that I knew that she was only using me, I would have been in heaven. She began to hug me, and kiss me in front of everyone. I actually felt strange about it, at first, especially in front of Dane. Before, I knew that he knew, that Shannon and I were doing it, but it was never in anybody's face.

But I got used to it. In fact, after a while, I began to let Shannon know that I liked it, grabbing her ass in public, which she hated. I'd say one of the most bizarre moments during this period, was the night at Dane's camp, when moans could be heard coming from behind the doors of two bedrooms, as Dane and Agnes, and Shannon and I, had each begun to approach our climaxes simultaneously.

During this time of dating Shannon exclusively, I had fallen more deeply in love with her than I'd ever been, despite believing that it was all just a ruse. One weekend, when her parents had gone out of town, she found herself able to spend the night with me, at my place. As we had begun to regain our composure after making love, I asked her to marry me. To my astonishment, she agreed.

The next day, without having told anyone, yet, we went to the jeweler, and she picked out an engagement ring, and wedding bands. It cleaned me out, but I didn't care. I was in a cloud. Somehow, this girl that I'd wanted all of my life had actually fallen in love with me. When we finally got around to telling Dane, later that day, I could see the look in his eyes. As far as he was concerned, I had broken the pact.

. . . . .

Almost immediately, I began to realize that this arrangement wasn't going to be easy. There was still something that I needed to know. It had been lingering in my mind for months, but when I asked Shannon to tell me about her big family secret, she refused.

"If we're gonna be married, we shouldn't keep things from each other," I nagged, and as I listened to myself saying it, I felt like an idiot.

"Some things are better left untold," she replied, and then she asked, "How do you know about it, anyway?"

I said, "Well Dane told me…"

And then I immediately felt like an idiot, again.

This revelation had really pissed her off.

She told me that there was nothing to it, and that, "Dane is a total moron! It's just another one of his ridiculous fireside ghost stories!"

I told her that I was sorry for bringing it up, and she seemed to calm down, after I assured her that I'd never ask her about it, again. But obviously, there was something behind it, and how did she know that what Dane had told me had involved anything to do with the supernatural? No matter what I had promised, I knew that the subject would, eventually come up, again.

I was sure that Shannon loved me. But she would never love me the way that she loved Dane. I could hear it in the tone of her voice when she called him a moron. The words had come more out of disappointment, than anger.

On the other hand, I could tell by her attitude towards me that I was simply being tolerated, and when I'd gotten a little too personal, I was shown that she was not going to tolerate much. She had agreed to marry me because I was willing to do it her way, and for the moment, she had thought that she'd lost to Agnes.

And why should Dane care about us getting hitched? He'd been trying to pawn Shannon off on me for months. He had his trophy girlfriend in Agnes. Even a blind man could see that he'd fallen hard for her, and she was far more compatible with him than Shannon ever could be.

Who was I trying to kid? Dane and Shannon might not be a perfect match, but they were meant for each other. Time would prove it. Nothing can stop time. Nothing can change fate. But like the love struck dummy that I was, I was gonna try.

19

I'd been sifting through the evidence from my dad's final investigation in Savannah. All of the seemingly paranormal stuff that had been happening over the last few months had made me think about it. Of course, I didn't need an excuse to watch the film of Beth and Susan going at it. Neither did Sluggo.

But even after getting my kicks watching that part of it, a couple more times, I began to become attracted to the actual spiritual side of it. Something had begun to draw me towards the house, itself.

I decided to talk the gang into taking a trip down there for a visit to Winter Winds. It wasn't hard to convince Dane. Neither one of the girls were thrilled by the idea of haunted houses, but a trip to a beautiful city like Savannah was enough to sway their vote.

Time had marched into the early weeks of April, and the weather had been unusually warm. We hadn't seen a snowflake, since February, and the temperatures hadn't dipped below the forties and fifties the whole month of March.

Part of the appeal for the trip for the girls was the possibility of going to the beach. In Savannah, they were already experiencing balmy seventy and eighty degree temperatures. For Dane, it was the allure of the open road. He decided that he and I would follow the others down on our Harleys.

We waited another week, so Shannon could arrange a long weekend from work. Agnes was on spring break, and she had no problem switching a few days of work, as well.

In the meantime, I contacted Phil Parsons, who spoke with the owner of the estate for me. This is where we hit a stumbling block. The owner was reluctant to give us permission, due to the tragic results of my father's last visit, and also the fact that we had no money to offer to seal the deal.

Shannon said that it was a sign that we shouldn't do it, but I couldn't be deterred that easy. Something wanted me to come to that house, and with each new difficulty that arose, the more determined I became.

As it turned out, the place was actually on the market, so I called my long lost Aunt Lee Ann, who happened to be a realtor, and who had become just interested enough in the paranormal, that she pulled some strings, and acquired us admittance, as prospective buyers.

Of course, I asked Phil to join us. The idea of having an experienced investigator on board made the situation a little more comfortable, and I knew that he would have felt slighted if I hadn't included him.

Actually, he was hesitant, at first, and he warned me that it might not be a good idea to enter the house at all. But with the intrigue of working with me, and the lure of the house, itself, he couldn't resist.

As we prepared to go, a chance visit by my cousin Brent, his erstwhile girlfriend Bethany, and his sister Stephanie, resulted in them being invited, as well. The three had recently started their own little paranormal group, and even Phil had felt that there was strength in numbers.

There had been just one other minor bump in the road to Savannah. When I told Shannon the details of the Stone family history, she immediately freaked out, and said that she wasn't going. She wouldn't explain why, but she just wasn't going.

It was Dane, who talked her back into it. The problem for me, was how he'd convinced her.

Good girl that Shannon was, she'd insisted on living at home with her parents, until we made our wedding vows official. So, I stopped over at Dane's house, unannounced, the night before we were scheduled to leave, to actually ask him to talk her into reconsidering the trip.

As I stepped up onto his porch, I could see through the front window that Shannon was almost completely undressed, and was in the process of removing Dane's pants, on the living room couch. Feeling much like a creeper, I quietly slipped away, undetected.

I did not want to see the girl I was soon to marry, making love to Dane. But I also realized that fair was fair. He had let me have Shannon when she was his. Now, I was to let him have her, while she was mine. I was finally beginning to understand the rules of the pact. Shannon didn't belong to either of us. We belonged to her.

· · · ·

As luck would have it, it poured down rain as we passed through the mountains of both West Virginia and Virginia. Needless to say it wasn't fun, but Dane and I had rain gear, and we toughed it out. The long haul on a motorcycle is hard on a body, anyway, not as bad for Dane, whose particular model of bike was bigger, and provided a little more comfortable ride.

Still it was a blast, and a few extra rest stops made it a breeze. Brent and Stephanie sniveled about all the stops, but when we told them to go on ahead of us, they calmed down, and got with the program. Shannon and Agnes, who rode together, actually had become quite chummy by the time we'd rolled on into the Savannah city limits.

We decided to seek lodging at a nice place, along I-95, because the hotels that are in the city, itself are all tourist attractions, all historical landmarks, and are all considered to be haunted. Needless to say, the accommodations are usually required to be booked in advance, and the rates aren't included in the economy package... So, while it would have been interesting to spend the night in a haunted hotel, it just wasn't in our budget.

A stroll through the city of Savannah is like taking a trip back in time. Very few buildings stand more than three or four stories tall. Spanish moss hangs, lazily from huge oak trees, providing shade to the courtyards and squares, which are scattered throughout town.

The city is full of history, having been directly involved in every major war that has taken place on American soil. Large sections of Savannah have been burned to the ground, no less than three times, and notably had been spared another, when upon its capture by General William Tecumseh Sherman, and his Union troops, the city was presented to President Lincoln as a Christmas present.

The whole city is said to be haunted. Once we'd settled in, and had a bite to eat, we walked around town, and almost every building that we had visited, boasted to having ghostly residents, or at least some sort of paranormal activity.

At a bar, well known for its spirits, we were led to the basement, where several of us were touched by unseen hands. A photo of a shadow figure was also captured, and the voice of someone saying, "Hello," was recorded on tape.

We ended the evening with a walk down River Street, where the party goes on almost every night, and the ghosts of shanghaied sailors are said to roam. The border of South Carolina lies just across, and beyond the banks of the Savannah River, which flows past, and into the Atlantic Ocean.

At one point, our view of the Carolina shoreline had become obscured by a huge cargo tanker, as it slowly passed, just arriving from Japan, or some other eastern seaport. It is not possible to experience all the city has to offer in one night, but we had business to attend to, anyway, and we were tired, so we drove back to our hotel for a good night's sleep.

. . . . .

In the morning, we met Phil Parsons, and then we headed for Winter Winds, where my Aunt Lee Ann had been waiting to give us the tour.

We had been forced to limit our investigation to the daytime hours, under our guise of being interested in buying the place, but Phil assured us that it didn't matter

According to him, "The residents of Winter Winds are ready, and willing to entertain guests, day or night."

Just as advertised, it was like going from day to night, walking through the front door of the house. It was eighty degrees outside, but once inside, you could see your breath, as if the temperature had dropped to freezing. I hadn't been in there five minutes, and already, I could understand why nobody wanted to live in the place. It was a tomb.

Amateurs that we were, we were not equipped with all of the sophisticated hardware that Phil had been used to, but he did manage to bring some of his own. We were able to place cameras in several areas of the house, and each team had access to night vision cameras and digital recording devices.

There was no central command center in which to monitor each teams' activities, so we were basically all on our own.

Phil thought that it was a dangerous way to investigate, but he went along with it, when I asked him, "Well, what in the hell did they do in the old days?"

Phil also asked Lee Ann if she'd like to stay and pair up with his team. Aunt Lee Ann wasn't exactly what you'd call hip, but she was no prude, either. My dad's exploits had made her think, and she had recently become more open minded.

She agreed, admitting that she'd had nothing better to do that afternoon, and that, "I was hoping you'd ask."

At first we split up into two teams. One comprised of Dane, Agnes, Shannon, and myself. The other with Phil, Lee Ann, Brent, Bethany, and Stephanie. Stephanie complained that she, her brother, and Bethany should be free to investigate on their own, but everyone agreed that it wouldn't be fair to Phil and Lee Ann to be by themselves.

The plan was, that each team would take one half of the house, and then after an hour or so, we would switch. The idea being that if one team should experience something, the other would try to replicate it.

The interior of the house was almost completely shrouded in darkness, despite the fact that we had barely reached the noontime hour of a brilliantly sunlit day. Dane, the girls, and I made our way through the shadowy halls armed only with flashlights, and a couple of night vision cameras.

After about forty-five minutes, we found the bedroom that sisters, Prudence and Temperance had shared.

We had been doing EVP sessions throughout our walk, immediately playing them back to listen for evidence, and there in what was known to have once been the girls' personal space, we asked the question, "Who lived in this room?"

The answer, "We did."

Shannon got up the nerve, and asked, "Who is we?"

To which you could clearly hear the voices of two girls answering simultaneously, "Temperance and Prudence."

The excitement between the four of us had begun to build, and when we listened to the next sequence, I swear each one of us almost shit our pants.

Shannon asked the question, "Temperance, why are you still here?"

The response, "Baby."

Dane asked, "Whose baby?"

The answer, "Mine."

"But ... what keeps you and your baby here?" he asked.

"Can't leave," came the response.

"Why, can't you leave?" Dane pressed.

"Father," the voice replied.

During that sequence of questions, Agnes and Shannon both had begun to squirm, and instinctively, the two had fallen into a protective embrace.

"Something was touching me," Shannon whimpered.

"Me too," Agnes chimed, almost sounding pleased.

Then she said, "Has anybody noticed how much colder it's gotten in here? I've never felt my nipples get this hard before."

Despite the situation that we were in, her blunt anatomical observation, immediately caused my dick to stiffen into a full erection. It wasn't hard for the rest of us to notice that Agnes was becoming visibly turned on. Now, at least two of us had begun to fall into a seemingly unprovoked state of sexual arousal.

What is going on here?

And then in the next moment, I wanted to lick Agnes' pussy, so badly, that I could swear I could smell the hypnotic scent of her sex through her clothing, and two feet away from her.

But just as quickly, the sound of Shannon's voice had snapped me out of it.

"Was that the ghost of Temperance Stone?" she asked.

To that, Dane looked at her in mock disbelief, and then he replied, "Does Pinocchio have wooden balls?"

The moment of levity sent each of us into a fit of nervous laughter. Our excitement at capturing an almost complete conversation with who we had believed to be the Stone sisters, had been almost impossible to contain.

After trying to get a few more responses, the interaction had ceased, and it seemed as though the Stone girls had left us. We all agreed that the temperature in the room had fallen dramatically, while the session had taken place, and had warmed up again, once our paranormal powwow had ended,

Each of us had naturally experienced the creeped out feeling of goosebumps. The hair rising from the skin. As we were leaving the room, Shannon and Agnes both admitted to feeling the sensation of having their breasts, and their genitals caressed, during the session.

Agnes, trying to whisper, even confessed to Shannon that she had become so wet, that the crotch of her panties was still soaked. I, on the other hand, hadn't completely lost my erection, and when I had overheard her very impenitent admission, my dick swelled right back up, again.

. . . . .

In the other half of the house, team number two had also been successful in recording a few ghostly messages from beyond. Only theirs hadn't been of the friendly kind.

When Phil asked if anyone was there with them, a man's voice told them to, "Get out."

Phil then asked the question, "Why are we not welcome?"

This time a woman's voice replied, "As good as dead," the part before it being muffled.

Each of those present agreed that it sounded like, "You're all, as good as dead."

In what would be the main living room, Bethany witnessed a full body apparition of a woman, dressed in Civil War era clothing.

When they asked the question, "Is that you, Petula Stone?" they received another stern response from what sounded like an angry man.

"Leave…" he warned.

Suddenly, all hell broke loose. A candelabra left the mantle of the fireplace on its own, and struck Phil on the back of his head, knocking him out, cold. A low rumble started in the foundation, and in seconds the whole house began to shake, as if about to crumble from the effects of an earthquake.

The walls began to heave, and the house began to tilt, and in what seemed like the blink of an eye, everyone became separated. Brent, Bethany, and Stephanie found themselves on the second floor balcony, heading towards the front hall, but when they'd reached the spot where they stairway should have been, they were to find that it had moved.

The great stairway hadn't fallen, it wasn't damaged. It had simply moved from the center of the front entrance, to the left side of the door, as you're coming into the house. The railing of the balcony, now continued past the spot where the summit of the stairs had been. It was as if someone had reconstructed the house in a matter of minutes.

The three pea green paranormal investigators were just forty feet from the front door, and had the freedom to follow Wilhelm Stone's orders, but they had found themselves bereft of the nerve to descend the twenty steps that it would take to get them there. For they did not know if this was some kind of illusion, or if they had been rendered bereft of their senses, as well.

.   .   .   .   .

Somehow, Shannon and Agnes wound up back in the bedroom of Temperance and Prudence Stone.

"What's going on? How did we get in here, again?" Shannon whispered, nervously.

"I don't know," Agnes replied, "but it's a bedroom, with a bed. Let's take advantage of it."

"Very funny."

"Why not, Shannon… You know you've been dying to get into my panties the past couple of days."

"What are you saying? You're crazy, ya know that?"

Agnes acted as if the comment hadn't registered. She began to lift her shirt over her head, revealing a lacy red bra, barely covering her gorgeous bosoms.

"Stop it, Agnes… I mean it! We have to figure out how to get out of here, and find the guys. Aren't you scared?"

Agnes' voice grew husky and direct, almost as if someone had been speaking through her, "It's what people know about themselves, inside, that makes 'em afraid, Shannon."

"Who are you?" Shannon replied, not even realizing the pertinence of the question.

Agnes began to remove her bra.

"Take off your clothes, Shannon… We haven't all afternoon, you know."

"She thinks I should undress for her," Shannon remarked, to no one in particular. "In the middle of a haunted house. No… I'm not going to undress for you, and I don't know what

the hell you think you're doing! Put your clothes back on...
I'm getting out of here!"

"But I like to take my clothes off, Shannon... I want to
take them off, right now..."

Agnes started to unbutton her pants, and when she did,
Shannon moved towards her, and tried to stop her.

"Agnes... No..."

"Let it happen, Shannon," Agnes soothed. "It has to happen."

Suddenly with those words, Shannon seemed to lose her resolve. She dropped her hands to her side, and let Agnes remove her shirt and bra. Agnes led her to the side of the bed,
placed her hands on Shannon's breasts, and gently pushed her
onto the silken sheets below.

Agnes followed her, and began to kiss her belly, her nipples, and finally her lips. Shannon wrapped her arms around
Agnes, and responded by shoving her tongue into Agnes'
mouth, breathing and moaning, as if fighting for her last
breath.

Agnes' hand went between Shannon's legs, feverishly ca-
ressing the hot spot that had quickly begun to grow impatient
for her touch. She unbuttoned Shannon's pants, and started to
tug at them, finding resistance at her thighs.

At this point, Shannon had no desire to stop Agnes from
undressing her, and she began to put everything she had into
stripping Agnes, too. Agnes moved away, and finished removing the denim prison that separated her from Shannon's soft,
warm skin, and then she helped Shannon wriggle out of hers.

The two women, now completely naked began to writhe
hungrily against each other, pawing and sucking each other's
breasts, feeding on each other's essence, as if the sustenance
meant the difference in whether they would survive the moment.

Shannon squirmed out from under Agnes, and took position on top of her. She began to grind herself into her, as if she
were fucking her, her body alternately undulating gently, and
then bucking, violently against her.

She reached between the two of them, and slowly inserted her fingers into Agnes' glistening sex. For a moment, Agnes became still, as if she had suddenly felt the desire to take the time to enjoy something that felt very good to her. Her eyes closed, and she slowly began to raise her hips to meet Shannon's teasing thrusts.

Shannon shoved her tongue into Agnes' belly button, and then she started to kiss and bite her way southward, until she was between her legs, biting her fig. She began to wipe her face into Agnes' wispy blond mound, her face becoming soaked with her juice.

By now Agnes' juice was smeared all over her thighs, and running down her leg. She reached down with both hands, and pulled herself open, as far as she could. Shannon hungrily attacked her, and began to suck the honey, right out of her hive.

Agnes began to come, and when Shannon was sure that she'd coaxed every bit of her climax from her, she positioned herself so that Agnes could lick her, too.

Agnes began to let her have it, and soon Shannon's juice was running down her leg, like a river. She began to bite Shannon's belly, and then she pushed her tongue deep into her split.

Muffled, breathless moans began to emanate from between both women's legs, and in another minute, Shannon's climax began to shudder through her body. A moment later, Agnes began to come, as well, and had her face not been squeezed firmly between Shannon's thighs, everyone in the house would have heard her.

. . . . .

I'd had no way of realizing it at the time, but I could have very well walked in on Shannon and Agnes, had I chosen the right door. The girls' bedroom was at the opposite end of the hall, and even though I'd thought that I had heard what sounded like moaning in the distance, I couldn't be sure if it had been human in nature, or spectral.

Instead, I turned, and entered into the bedroom of Wilhelm and Petula Stone. In some sort of a trance, I had been pulled towards the room, and once inside, I discovered my Aunt Lee Ann standing alone, at the foot of the bed.

At first, she looked bewildered and scared, "Joshua... What just happened? How did we get here?"

"I don't know," I replied, "but we'd better find the others."

I went to her, and took her hand, and as I turned to leave, she held fast to where she stood.

"Wait, Joshua... Don't leave me," she pouted. The look on her face had changed. She smiled, sheepishly, and then her eyes seemed to travel up and down my body, as if she were checking me out.

I let go of her hand, "Come on," I said, and as I began to move towards the door, she called to me, the sound of want in her tone.

When I turned again to her, she was still smiling, but now, it had evolved into a smile wrought with lust. She began to unbutton her blouse, and it was then that I realized that she hadn't been wearing a bra.

Then, I remembered that she had been wearing a t-shirt, before. This was not her blouse that she was wearing. It dawned on me that the style was that of 1800's period clothing.

Whose clothing?

Her breasts tumbled out, from beneath their cover, her nipples erect. Her shirt, lay on the floor as she began to move towards me. I moved past her to retrieve the blouse, but by the time I had picked it up, and turned to cover her, she had already quickly begun to advance towards me.

Lee Ann swooped upon me like a vampire, to its prey. Her eyes were red as fire. Her breath caressed me like a drug. Her hand dropped, and closed on my quickly swelling rod. She squeezed it, gently, teasingly, but there was no teasing in her voice.

"We belong together, Joshua."

This wasn't my aunt talking. I pulled away, embarrassed that I'd hardened, but she continued to pursue me, this time in an embrace that within seconds, I was unwilling to escape.

She pressed her lips to my face, her tongue hungrily searching for mine. All modesty had left me. I was consumed with lust.

I pushed her onto the bed and devoured her, this woman who was twice my age. Our pants never made it past our ankles. I entered her, hard, her split enveloping my entire length. A momentary cry of pain escaped her, and then the guttural moans of a predator, hungry to be nourished.

It was the hardest, fastest fuck, I'd ever had. Our bodies burning, soaked with sweat, the place where our genitals coupled, engulfed in flames. I felt as though I would never reach orgasm, and I didn't care if I had to hurt her to achieve it. I couldn't stop myself. The more I thought about it, the deeper I would push.

There was a moment when I had turned my head, and saw the figure of a woman, standing at the foot of the bed, watching us. I looked into her eyes, but there was no recognition in her expression that she had even noticed. She only seemed to be interested in Lee Ann.

Suddenly, I began to come with such force, that I thought I was gonna split in two. Lee Ann's moaning turned to a scream that sounded as though she was being torn from the inside out, and then she passed out beneath me, as her climax shuddered to a stop.

I had no idea how much time had passed, but I could feel Lee Ann clinging to me, trembling. When she saw that I had noticed her, she pulled her pants up, and left me, without saying a word. No one saw her leave the house.

. . . . .

For me, Winter Winds had definitely lived up to its reputation. I certainly didn't need any documented proof to convince myself, but I did collect all of the tapes, especially the one from the master bedroom. No one had seen or heard anything that had happened in that room, and I aimed to keep it that way.

I wasn't exactly sure what all was on that tape, because, at some point, the camera had malfunctioned, lost power, and turned itself off. How long it had been off, I did not know, but I did have to wonder, had Wilhelm Stone not wanted anyone to see it, as well?

What had happened to Lee Ann and myself in that room had thrown me for a loop. I'm certain that I hadn't completely been myself in there, and neither had Lee Ann. Someone or something had taken partial control of our thoughts and emotions, and may have also used our bodies to experience a physical connection that could no longer be achieved in the spiritual realm.

Who the woman was that had been in the room with us, I did not know, but I would be willing to guess that it had been Petula Stone. As to who had been the orchestrator of our torrid supernatural tryst, I had no doubt in my mind that it had been none other than Wilhelm Stone, himself.

Anyway, everyone had managed to make it out of the house in one piece. The only ones that had seemed to be really shook up from the experience were the paranormal three, Brent, Bethany, and Stephanie, who had thrown caution to the wind, and had taken the detour down the misplaced stairway, and right out the front door. They did not stick around after we'd vacated the house, choosing to head back to Pennsylvania, immediately.

Dane had found Phil in the basement, a little woozy and confused, but the gash on his head turned out to be little more than a scratch to a grizzled veteran such as he, and nothing that a couple of stitches wouldn't cure. Phil made me promise to send him copies of the tapes, which of course I would, all except the one.

As with every other strange event that had occurred that afternoon, the phenomenon of the great stairway having changed its position in the house, was put down to having been some sort of physical manifestation brought on by mass hypnotic suggestion, for as we were leaving the house, we were all comforted to note that it had safely returned to its rightful position in the front hall.

As we locked the front doors, we all agreed that none of us would ever return to Winter Winds, the general consensus being that one afternoon visit with the Stone family was enough of a memory to last a lifetime. It was also agreed upon that there was presently, and probably always would be, a very evil entity presiding in the house, and for everyone's sake, the place should be burned to the ground, and that nothing should ever be built on the property, again.

Strangely, though a little shook up from their experience at Winter Winds, Shannon and Agnes appeared to be becoming cozier and cozier, as our stay in Savannah progressed. Since we'd arrived in town, the two of them, who up until then had not cared much for each other, at all, had seemed as if they had worked out their differences.

At the time no one knew exactly what had happened to them in that room, myself included, because they weren't talking. They would only admit that something unexplainable had occurred, and that for a period of time, they had both drifted in and out of consciousness, to the point where they had very little recollection of how they had wound up together in bed, and very naked.

It did seem to me that the incident had brought them closer, still, almost as if it had provided a positive experience for them. It did not escape my senses, that in conveying the fact that she and Agnes had somehow found themselves in bed, and in their birthday suits, that there had been a distinct tone of pleasure in Shannon's voice.

It had become plain to see by both Dane and myself that Shannon and Agnes, who had once been mortal enemies, had become the best of friends in a matter of days. Dane had seemed pleased by their union.

"Now we can all hang out without drama," he'd remarked.

Me, I wasn't so sure. I suspected their friendship to be something more, and I saw it as a sign of trouble on the horizon.

Later that night, my suspicions were satisfied, when upon returning to the hotel from a beer run, I was treated to the shock of seeing Agnes and Shannon locked in a passionate embrace, as the doors of the elevator they'd been using opened into the lobby. I quickly hid myself from their view, and they did not notice me, as they proceeded, hand in hand, towards the front doors of the building, on their way for an evening stroll of the hotel grounds.

In bed that night, as Shannon lay sleeping peacefully by my side, I couldn't help but picture in my mind what kind of stroll, she and Agnes had taken earlier in the evening. Was it under the cover of branches from a low hanging tree, or had they found a patch of bushes that could possibly hide them from the prying eyes of others? Maybe, they had simply used the car.

The next day, we went to the beach to satisfy the girls, and later, after stuffing ourselves at a really good hamburger joint, we hit River Street. All four of us got so disgustingly drunk, that we had to sleep in the car, where at some point in the night, Shannon puked all over my lap.

At dawn, we drove back to the hotel, showered up, packed our things, and began the long ride back to Pittsburgh. We caught the rain in the mountains, just as we had on the way down, the only notable difference being that at one point, we found ourselves sitting still in a traffic jam heading into Virginia, where a tractor trailer loaded with pigs inched its way along side of us, for what seemed like eternity. The smell was lovely.

Conveniently, Dane and I were able to move ahead, and escape the stench by traveling down the shoulder of the road. Hence, the beauty of riding on two wheels.

20

Masturbation [mas-ter-**bəy**-shən] n. 1. The simulation or manipulation of one's own or another's genitals to achieve orgasm.

I couldn't wait to view the footage of Agnes and Shannon, once I'd returned home, and had gotten some rest. I did try to watch it with an investigative mindset, but as things progressed, I became aware that this footage seemed far more erotic than the film of Beth and Susan. Obviously these two girls really turned me on.

Maybe it was because I had been close to the both of them, and had made love with each of them myself, but almost unconsciously, I had opened my pants, just as they had in the film, and had begun to coax myself into an erection. As the two of them made love, I let myself feel as though I was right there between them, and soon, Shannon began to quiver, and Agnes began to squirm, and in another moment, the three of us were beginning to…

As I watched the tape over and over, I began to get the feeling that something really was different about these two girls. Something just didn't fit. First of all, their experience had occurred in a room other than where this phenomenon had usually taken place, and while Agnes had definitely assumed the role of seductress, it seemed as though she had been begging Shannon more than anything else.

As for Shannon, she seemed to be fighting something alright, but to me it looked as though she had simply been resisting urges that she'd been wrestling with long before she had ever entered that room.

Something may have been nudging the girls along, but to me it hadn't looked at all as though they had been forced to do anything against their will. By the end of the third viewing of this particular footage, I had become convinced that the actions between these two women had been completely consensual.

.   .   .   .   .

It had been about a week since we'd returned from Savannah, that I began to wonder if we'd left Winter Winds with a price on our heads. For even though I'd begun to think that something was amiss, I could have never, in a million years predicted the chain of events that would happen next.

For starters, just as Agnes had come back into Dane's life, completely out of the blue, for some inexplicable reason, she turned right back around, and left him. Of course, I assumed it was to be with Shannon. Boy, was I wrong.

The turn of events had really shaken Dane up. He had fallen for Agnes.

"I don't understand it, Bro," he said, in a voice that had clearly had the wind knocked out of it, "I seriously thought she was the one."

It was plain to see that his confidence level had taken a direct hit. The poor guy had found himself in a state of total bewilderment.

Naturally, he went straight to Shannon, seeking comfort, which was no surprise, but what he did next was completely out of character. He begged Shannon to take him back. When she reminded him that she had been engaged to me, he did something else that I'd never expect from him. He told Shannon about Ranae.

And of course, Shannon immediately dumped me. Now, it was me doing the begging. I assured her that there had been no proof that the kid was mine. I reminded her that my fling with Ranae had been long before we'd become engaged, and had been ancient history.

"That doesn't matter!" she cried. "You promised that you would only be with me! You promised that you'd only make love to me! You wanted to get me pregnant! You had to get somebody pregnant!"

What could I say? She had a solid case against me. I knew that I wasn't going to change her mind. Her mind had already been made up long before Dane had told her about Ranae. He had simply dropped the out that she'd been looking for, directly into her lap. The whole thing had been a farce, anyway. Me and Shannon married... what a laugh.

Actually, I cried. I'd just lost the girl that I had dreamed about my whole life. That I'd had her for that short period of time was the dream. What did I have to snivel about anyway? Shannon had been giving herself to me all along, and I had to remember that I'd never had her to begin with. She'd had me.

Anyway, once Shannon had dumped me, she openly began to go after Agnes. She had fallen in love with her. But Agnes began to play hard to get. She made Shannon beg for her. Then Agnes told her to take a hike. Shannon was devastated. Agnes disappeared.

It was then that I realized, that from the moment that she had picked me up in the Hotel, that night, a few months back, Agnes had begun to initiate an act of total revenge, against Dane, Shannon, and myself. She got Dane for dumping her for Shannon. She got Shannon for taking Dane from her. And, she got me for that night at the party, so long ago.

That was the best part. That this had been stewing inside of her, for all that time. That she had waited for just the right moment in order to inflict the most pain. The only thing that would have made it sweeter, was if she'd been able to get to Sara, too.

Sara... My love... Is all of this good enough for you? I hope so. I also hope that Shannon still has her friend Peter lying around, 'cause I have the feeling that for the next few days, she's gonna need him. Dane has his photo gallery... I've got my films, which I like to call "Supernatural Slumber Party, Parts One and Two." I'd be willing to say that if the three of us were to make a bet on who could hold out the longest, Shannon would probably win. I'm pretty sure that I wouldn't.

21

The ironic part of it was that Agnes hadn't even known about Ranae. She had been counting on her seduction of Shannon to be the thing that would break us up. Dane's indiscretion in telling Shannon had simply been the icing on the cake.

Meanwhile, Ranae was still mad at me. She was about to give birth to a kid that was almost certainly mine. I wasn't trying to be a dick, but I had continued to insist that we get proof. I liked the idea of having a kid, but even though she assured me that I had been the only one during the time she got knocked up, I knew better. I hate to say it, but Ranae was that kind of girl.

So, the more that I insisted, the more she resisted, and the more she resisted, the less I believed her. So, she said that she couldn't be with a guy who didn't trust her, and I said that I couldn't trust a girl who couldn't do one simple thing to make me happy.

The sad part of it was, that if she had just agreed to do it, I would've been content. She would've had me, and then that would've made her happy. I wasn't in love with her, but I did like her, and what the hell, I didn't have any other prospects, at the moment. I was beginning to give in.

But I wasn't looking forward to dealing with Miles over it, either. He made it simple. He came to me, and told me that he was leaving Ranae. He admitted that Echo wasn't his kid. He said that he was tired of dealing with her. He told me that I was doing him a favor, that he'd been waiting for something like this to happen. He said that he couldn't stand Ranae, and that if he had even liked her a little bit, he would have killed me, a long time ago.

Miles was gone that night. Two days later, Ranae gave birth to a baby boy. I don't think the kid ever got a name. Ranae jumped out of a third story window in the hospital. They didn't need to send an ambulance. She was dead on arrival.

Miles never came back. I took a test. The kid wasn't mine. Echo went into the system. Ranae came to me in a dream. She cut off my balls. I screamed, and then Stormy woke me up. I still had my balls. Ranae was still dead.

. . . . .

It was during this time that Dane started to bounce from woman to woman. In another one of her strange moods, Shannon had made herself scarce, and neither Dane nor myself had been seeing much of her. Dane took a ride to Gettysburg to see Gabrielle, who, as he put it, had been so glad to see him that she led him directly to the bedroom from the front door. But after three days, things had cooled down between them, again, and Dane came back home.

Then Dane began to see Brent's on and off again girlfriend, Bethany, which made Brent's sister, and my cousin Stephanie, extremely jealous. I guess Stephanie had been hot for Dane for a while, but he just hadn't been interested in her.

Stephanie had always been a little jealous of me, too. As kids, I used to play strip poker with her, and just around the time that we'd both begun to reach the awkwardness of puberty, I began my quest to devirginize her. She'd had no qualms about letting me succeed.

A while before Shannon and I had ever come out of the closet, Stephanie had figured us out. One night at a party, she came right out, and called me on it.

She had been bad mouthing Shannon, and when I started to stick up for her, Stephanie suddenly blurted, "You're fucking her, aren't you!?"

I almost fell over from the viciousness in her voice. Even Bethany was shocked.

"Stephanie!" she admonished.

I denied it, of course, but I began to think...

What would make her say that? How could she know?

So I asked her.

She said, "I can tell by the way you look at her. I can tell by the way you talk about her. I can see it when the two of you are together... The way she looks at you!"

Geez, is it that obvious?

But she had hit a nerve, and I tore into her. I told her to mind her own business, and to start worrying about her own fucked up life. Her life wasn't really fucked up, but it had sounded good at the time.

Stephanie had become so pissed, that she started to cry, and then she said, "It's time for me to go home."

I followed her outside, and told her that I was sorry. I gave her a hug, and then before I could stop myself, I had kissed her right on the lips. Our mouths opened, and her tongue began to beg mine for approval. She got it.

Later, after Stephanie had fallen asleep, I began to think about how Shannon had been able to pull different emotions from different people, to the point of obsession. I had become obsessed with love for her, because that's what love really is, an obsession. I had just never realized how obsessed with jealousy, Stephanie had become towards her.

Anyway, to come back to my present point, Stephanie and I, had suddenly taken up where we'd left off that night. Now, it was the two of us that had begun to sneak around. I don't know why. Our familial connection fell way down the hereditary line. Maybe, it had been because for the both of us, it had merely been a fling, and unlike my father, I had no intention of ever marrying my cousin.

By the time that things had cooled down with me and Stephanie, Dane had dumped Bethany for another girl named Bobbie Jo Hatfield. As a kid, she had always been referred to, as Tubby Hatfield's little sister. Now, she was all grown up, and very hot. There was just one catch. She had gotten knocked up at the age of sixteen, and still lived with the father.

Dane and I had started playing, again as Finger Pickin' Good, and we had acquired a spot on Thursday nights at a club called The Canteen, which was located in the basement of a bowling alley. The combination of the location, the size, and the ambiance of the place presented the feel of a coffee house that served alcohol.

Bobbie Jo worked there as a server, and it wasn't long before she and Dane had started an affair. It was the same old story. She told Dane that she was tired of a boyfriend who no longer paid any attention to her. She said that she planned on leaving him. Dane fell hard for her.

I warned him that the ending wasn't gonna be the one that he was hoping for. I told him that the boyfriend was gonna find out, and that he wasn't going to be happy. I assured him that she wouldn't leave the guy, but he didn't listen. After about a month, she got tired of Dane, and she started acting aloof, and then cold. Eventually, Dane got the picture.

. . . . .

Dane and I had both been having our ups and downs with women, but what happened to me next had to have beaten it all. I did not want to answer my phone that day, since I had been nursing a mind splitting hangover, and had been praying for an early death. But I did answer my phone, and let me say, death would have been preferable.

"Joshua, we have a problem."

"Not as bad as the one we were having when I last saw you. It's good to know you're still alive. So... what is the problem?"

"I'm pregnant."

"What do you mean... you're pregnant?"

"I mean, I'm pregnant."

"You're forty-something, you can't be pregnant. Do you and Wayne even do it, anymore?"

"I'm telling you, I'm knocked up, and it isn't Wayne's."

"So what are you telling me?"

"Really, Joshua! You can't be that stupid... Duh!"

"How do you know it's mine?"

"The timing... Again, duh!"

"Maybe it's Stone's. You and him were lookin' pretty cozy at the end there."

"You son of a bitch!"

"Look, what do you want from me? You seduced me. I can't be held responsible for some supernatural sex romp. Neither of us can. How would it look, you having your nephew's kid? You'd have to kiss Liz's ass for the rest of your life. Hey, what we did was pretty kinky... Maybe, deep down you'd like to kiss Liz's ass!"

Click.

Me to myself in the mirror, "You're shit. You're lower than shit. Whatever is lower than shit... that's what you are."

My life was falling apart.

I couldn't even say, "Why me?" because I knew that I was to blame for it all.

"I'm not a good person," I told myself. "I can lie to myself and to everyone else, and, if there is a hell... which I hope there isn't... I'm sure I own a first class ticket to the front gate."

I eventually called Lee Ann back, and apologized. I told her that I was sorry for getting her into the whole mess. She said that the only reason that she had called me, was that she thought it was only fair for me to know that I had put a child on this earth, but that she hoped that I'd stay out of it, and let her raise the kid as hers and Wayne's.

She said that she would make Wayne think the child was his, because, "I could never tell him that gawd awful story."

She said that she figured that the kid would be better off never even seeing me, lest the curse that had obviously been handed down from my father, rub off on another generation.

Her plea had made sense to me, so I promised her that I'd respect her wishes, and leave them alone. I just hoped for Lee Ann's sake that it was my kid, because the alternative might possibly turn her life into a living hell.

.   .   .   .   .

The things that Lee Ann had said, had stuck in my mind, so I had to ask myself, "Could I be cursed? And, if I am, did it start with my father, or is it something that had taken place way back when in the old country?"

At any rate, the similarities between my father and myself were beginning to mount. The funny thing is, that even though my father had been the big ghost hunter, it is my mother, who possesses the ability to communicate with spirits.

She once admitted to me that her abilities had fallen somewhere between where I am at, and those of a full-blown medium. She said that the more you practice it, or let it happen, the stronger it gets. She told me that once the dead realize that you know they are there, they will start to bug you because they think you can help them. She said that it's not easy, but she avoids it altogether, and that she just turns it off if it begins.

She advised me to stop all of the ghost hunting, even for fun, because you don't know what you're dealing with on the other side, and you could possibly be inviting pure evil to enter into our realm.

Maybe my mother can simply shut it off, but it's not that easy for me. I just don't know how to do it. I'd been seeing spirits in my house, again. I'd seen Brigid several times, and each time, she'd shown herself in a more progressive state of decomposition.

Then, one night, someone climbed into bed with me. I watched the covers ripple, and the shape of another body form beneath them. Though physically, I could not feel anything solid, I could definitely feel a presence, and even though it had been quite warm in the house, it had suddenly become ice cold under the sheets. The clincher was that I could smell Ranae's perfume.

I believe that she is now one of the spirits hanging out at the store, as well. I can smell her perfume constantly and there has been an increase in things being moved around. Lately, I've been hearing the sound of a woman crying.

Otis the drunk had come into the store one day, shortly after her passing, and as he was pouring himself a cup of coffee, an empty cup fell from the stack, and onto the floor. He picked it up, and tried to hand it to someone, who wasn't there. When I asked him what he was doing, he said that there had been a woman there, who was having trouble getting a coffee cup. He said that when he had tried to help her, she'd disappeared right in front of him.

Now, you could put that down as Otis being a drunk, and simply seeing things, but when I asked him to tell me what she'd looked like, he described Ranae.

22

It had started out to be a good day, really, it did. Dane had called and asked me to come over.

"Bring some beer," he added.

I brought the beer and a couple of steaks to go with it. After grilling the steaks, I suggested that we go down to the Hotel, because I wanted to introduce him to Stormy. I had been talking him up to her, and she wanted to meet him. Basically, I was just trying to help him forget about all of his woman troubles, by getting him into more woman trouble.

But we never made it to the Hotel. Dane had received a couple of phone calls, and had begun to make a few, himself. When I asked him what was up, he told me that Bethany and Stephanie wanted to go ghost hunting. I had really wanted him to meet Stormy, but I figured, what the hell, we'll go hang out at the cemetery, get the girls good and scared, and then let them have their way with us.

But I was wrong, because the next thing I knew, Erin had showed up. She had been hanging around with Bethany and Stephanie, lately, and had been under the impression that we were all going to see a movie. Not only had she been mistaken, but she'd been misled as well. The other girls had both known that Erin was not into ghost hunting. Not just not into it, she was afraid of it.

Erin is a good girl, but to hang out with the older girls meant a lot to her.

"Why would they invite her along, and then pull this on her?" I fumed.

That had pissed me off, and to me, the night was already fucked. Then, Dane informed me that Shannon and her sister Rowen were coming.

"What...!? Why on earth would Shannon want to do this!" I marveled.

See, Dane and Shannon had begun to see each other, again, even though they were still officially broke up. Some people just couldn't get it. Bethany had fallen hard for Dane, and had been playing the role of the woman scorned, who'd been callously tossed aside by her heartless lover. Stephanie had taken it upon herself to become her defender, and the two girls had grown to absolutely loathe Shannon.

Inviting Shannon along was a huge mistake. For her, it would be like walking into the center of the enemy camp, defenseless. Like sitting on a powder keg that only needed a match. A disaster waiting to happen. I was sure that Shannon had no idea that the other girls would be there.

I begged Dane to forget about it. I told him to think of Erin. I told him to think of Shannon. He was determined. He wanted this to happen. I should have went home. But you know, it's like seeing a train wreck about to happen. As horrible as you know it's gonna be, you just can't look away.

So, Shannon showed up with Rowen. I like Rowen, and I'd always wanted her to hang out with us.

Maybe, since Rowen's here, they'll try to be on good behavior.

Wrong, again.

Erin was pissed, that she'd been duped and at that point in time, she'd grown to have very little patience or sympathy for Shannon. I told her that she and I could go see a movie.

"Oh no!" the others whined. "You have to come... Erin has to come!"

I assured Erin that I would be there with her, and that I would protect her. She reluctantly agreed.

Meanwhile, Bethany and Stephanie had been totally ignoring Shannon and Rowen, and so had Dane. How rude could they be? Well, they were just getting warmed up. It had become the norm for them to treat Shannon like shit, but why Rowen? Instead of trying to make her feel welcome, they went out of their way to show her what a bunch of smoldering assholes they could be.

I'd assumed that we would go to the usual haunts, but Stephanie had found a new place out in the middle of bumfucked nowhere. Dane, Shannon, Rowen, and I made the trip in Dane's van. Stephanie, Bethany and Erin took Stephanie's car. I'm usually good with directions, but I had no idea where we had been, because Rowen and I had spent the entire ride making out in the back of the van.

I had never realized that Rowen was such a friendly girl, but in the hour that it had taken us to reach our destination, I discovered that with two fingers, I could make her come twice, and in the process, almost have my ear bitten off.

Once we'd arrived, ahem, I mean once we had found the place, the mood quickly changed. Nobody could be sure if we were even in the right spot. We were looking for a supposed haunted tunnel on an old railroad line that had been converted into a walking trail, where supposedly, a railroad brakeman had been crushed between a couple of rail cars, and was now forever doomed to haunt the tunnel.

Well, we were on a trail, but we hadn't the faintest idea how far of a walk it might be in order to reach the tunnel, and it was really dark. We had only traveled a few hundred feet, when Shannon and Rowen decided that they did not want to go any farther, and that they just wanted to go home. That's when all hell broke loose.

At that point, everyone but Erin was pretty drunk. Stephanie argued that after coming as far as we had to get there, that there was no way that we were leaving.

Shannon said, "Fine, we'll walk."

We were forty miles from home, nobody was walking. I suggested that we go, since it was so late.

I tried to reason that, "Now that we know where this place is at, we can come back another time."

"We wouldn't have to leave if we didn't have to babysit these two losers!" Stephanie countered.

That's when I offered to drive Shannon and Rowen home. I figured that it would solve the problem, and after our clandestine dalliance in the back of the van, I had begun to have visions of bringing Rowen, and maybe even Shannon back to my place, anyway. Without hesitation, Dane threw me the keys to his vehicle.

The strange part was, that the whole time all of this was going on, Dane was saying nothing. He was just watching it happen, almost like an outsider, enjoying the show. I just didn't get it. I'd assumed that he and Shannon had been trying to work things out between themselves. Why had he turned on her like this?

So, Shannon, Rowen, and I turned around, and began to head back down the path. Shannon had been hanging on me the whole time. I wasn't sure if she was genuinely scared, or simply trying to make Dane jealous. She had never been overly scared on any other ghost hunts, unless you count that night in Gettysburg, but I felt like she was again using me to get to him. All of the way back to the van, she'd stuck to me like glue. Even Rowen had begun to look at her kind of funny, as if she too had begun to succumb to the jealous bone.

I could see Rowen being nervous. Here she was on a dark, spooky, and possibly dangerous trail at two in the morning, with a bunch of people that she really didn't know, who had already been acting hostile towards her and her sister. Now, Shannon had begun to draw my attention away from her, the only person who had shown her anything even slightly resembling kindness the whole evening.

Anyway, I had just slid the key into the ignition when Rowen said, "Here they come."

I looked up to see the rest of the gang loping towards us with such a pointed sense of urgency that if I hadn't known better, I'd have thought that we were about to be lynched.

Apparently, they had discussed it, and the general consensus had been that I was not to leave.

"Joshua, don't go!" Erin begged. "You promised that you would protect me."

"You've got a big brother," I countered.

Then I told her that she should just come home with us.

"But I don't want to," she said, a touch of coyness in her tone. "Everyone made me come out here, now I want to see what happens."

Stephanie had climbed into her car, and started to cry.

"I've been waiting to find this place for a long time. I finally find it, and now everybody is ruining it!"

Did you ever notice that when a drama queen is in the process of pointing blame, she always uses the word everybody, instead of confronting the person that she really has the problem with?

Bethany just stood there smoking a cigarette, and quietly observing the fallout with her usual dumb look on her face, and Dane stood next to her, still not saying a word. At this point, I had begun to get a little pissed at him. No matter what problems he and Shannon were having, it was he who should have stuck up for her. Instead, he'd thrown her to the wolves.

And, just like that night in Gettysburg, Shannon proceeded to put it all on me.

She began to cry, almost hysterically, and then she blurted, "Joshua, why don't you say something? Please... get some fucking balls, and stick up for me!"

"Oh...my...gawd..." Erin wailed, "what a fucking drama queen!"

That's when Rowen started to cry.

"Why can't everybody just be friends!?"

Good question, Rowen. I felt bad for her, but at the moment, I couldn't feel much compassion for Shannon. The whole thing had been a load of bullshit. Why had she decided to leave, just as we had come so close to reaching our destination? Why had she come at all? Had she been counting on this to happen, and if so, then why?

Anyway, I'd had it. It was time for me to make a decision. It was then that I became a coward. It was then that I proved to Shannon that I did not have a full set of balls. I knew that even if I would stick up for her this night, tomorrow she would run straight to Dane. I got out of the car, and Erin ran up and hugged me.

After Shannon and Rowen had left, we continued back down the trail. We found the tunnel not more than a couple hundred yards from where we had stopped the first time. As we entered the darkened corridor, Erin immediately freaked out, and refused to go any farther.

While I kept her company, Dane and the girls made their way through the tunnel, pausing midway, in order to conduct an EVP session. After awhile, they continued on to the other end, to listen to the results, and take a smoke break.

"What are they doing?" Erin whimpered.

"Having fun," I assured her.

"This is not fun," she corrected.

"Why did you come?" I asked.

"Because I'm an idiot, okay?"

I knew better than to comment on that one, but it wasn't long before I began to hear footsteps all around us. There were noises in the tunnel, and I could hear whispering. I knew that Erin heard it, too.

I said, "Did you hear that?"

She begged me not to talk. I guess she thought that if we spoke, the spirits would know that we were there. Well, let me tell you, they knew that we were there, because someone or something had begun to throw pebbles at us. I had to take Erin farther down the path.

After about a half an hour, Dane and the girls had returned, disappointed that nothing had happened around them. When I told them what Erin and I had experienced it only served to heighten their resolve. Erin was more than ready to leave, and so was I, but now Dane wanted to stay and explore another tunnel, that had crossed just underneath the trail that we had been on, and was still an operating railroad line.

The hillside appeared to be tough to descend, very steep with no path, but Dane had to check it out, and of course, so did Bethany. So, while the two of them carefully worked their way down the hill, Stephanie and I listened to the recorder once again, in case they had missed something. What we eventually heard, shocked us.

They had decided to leave the recorder on, as they made their way back through the tunnel, and most of what we heard could easily be identified as their own footsteps, and their own voices.

But after about a minute into the recording, another voice could be heard, beneath theirs that had clearly said, "Hey, come back."

Stephanie was thrilled, I was tired, and Erin was disgusted. Dane and Bethany had been in that tunnel for forty-five minutes. We all knew what was going on. Bethany is a nice girl, but she's as flaky as they come, hot to trot, and she was completely in love with Dane. Stephanie had felt triumphant. She had managed to squash her opponent, if only for the time being.

Dane had managed to get himself laid, and make Bethany a happy woman, again, if only for the time being, and even though I could care less, I did manage to find it humorous that when the two of them had finally come back up to the trail, Dane had naturally been wearing his poker face, but poor Bethany couldn't help but display an expression that had clearly radiated complete post-coital satisfaction.

. . . . .

It was a busy night at the Hotel, and the scene looked promising. The place was jumping, a treasure trove of beautiful girls. Stormy was already half drunk, enjoying a rare evening on the other side of the bar. I called Dane, and asked him to meet me. I told him that there were a lot of hot, available women in the vicinity, and that Stormy was one of them.

As I sat there, a line of girls came weaving their way through the crowd, and smack dab in the middle, I could swear that I saw Ranae dancing along with them. She looked at me and smiled, and seemed to be having a great time, but as she disappeared into a wall of people with the rest of the girls, I couldn't be sure if it had been her spirit that I had just seen, or simply a combination of her memory and the guilt that had been playing on my mind.

About a half an hour later, Dane showed up with Shannon, right behind him. I almost fell off my barstool. Now, I really thought that I was seeing things. I just could not fathom how after what had went on that night at the trail, how the two of them could have possibly recovered from it. They looked happy as clams. I knew then that I had indeed lost my mind. Then, Dane told me that Shannon wanted to go ghost hunting, just the three of us. How could I refuse?

We drove to one of our usual spots. All the while I could not help but notice how self-assured and happy Shannon seemed to be. She was in a really good mood to be sure. Once there, we climbed out of the van, and basically just stood around talking. We had no equipment, so this investigation had obviously been meant for the three of us to spend a warm summer evening, on a lovely country road, drinking a beer and enjoying each other's company.

When I said that I thought I'd seen a shadow figure near the back of the van, Shannon became uptight, and Dane implored me to stop scaring her.

Gee, why is he so concerned about her this night?

Dane and I started to have our usual debate about whether shadow people are evil, or not. I believe that shadow entities are not human spirits, and that no one knows where they come from. I explained to the two of them, that they are usually associated with poltergeist activity, and that it's possible that they could be intent on doing harm.

The next thing I knew, Dane started trying to scare Shannon, by telling her that he'd heard a growl in the woods, only a few yards from us. Within seconds, Shannon was hanging all over me, and Dane seemed as though he didn't mind it at all. As a mater of fact, he appeared to be quite pleased.

I just couldn't understand the two of them. One minute they'd seem fine together, and then in the matter of a moment's time, they would repel each other like oil and water.

· · · · ·

A few weeks later, I called Shannon, and asked her to stop over to my house, because I had a book that I wanted to give her. She agreed, and told me that she'd actually had something that she wanted to talk to me about, as well. I had assumed that she'd been referring to the night at the tunnels, but when I brought up the subject, only minutes after she'd arrived, she told me that she didn't want to talk about that, and as a matter of fact, thought it best to just forget about it.

I agreed to honor her wishes, but I did tell her that I was sorry about the whole thing, and I asked her to apologize to Rowen for me. Then I changed the subject, and we talked about the book for a while. She seemed to be genuinely interested, as she always is to talk about literature, but I could tell that there was something else that she had been wrestling with inside, and had been unsure of how to broach the subject.

"Okay, sweetheart," I prodded, as gently as I could. "What's worrying that pretty little head of yours?"

"First of all, I am not pretty. Kittens and puppies are pretty," she admonished.

"Right," I corrected myself. "I meant… that beautiful head of yours."

"That's better," she smiled, but then the smile left her face.

She stood up, and came over to me, wiping the tears that had begun to roll down her face. She lifted her dress and lowered her panties, just enough so that it was possible to have a clear view of the mound of fur just above her genitals. She parted her pubes to reveal a two-inch scar, located a few inches above her clitoris.

"This is the reason that I don't want to shave," she sobbed. "My mother gave me this scar with a huge knife, in some sort of devil ritual when I was thirteen. My father and my mother would lay me on a bed in the attic, that was made up to be some kind of an altar for sacrificial rites to be performed. It was to get favors from the Devil, or something. They did the same thing to Rowen, and the both of them raped us over and over, again. I resisted, but Rowen just gave into them, so they quit doing it to me, and Rowen became their special child. After awhile, they stopped doing it altogether, and then they acted as if it had never happened, and Rowen and I have done the same, since."

What she had just told me had boggled my mind.

What seemingly normal parents could be capable of doing this to their kids?

I just didn't know what to say. What words could I say that could possibly comfort her after having to admit something like that? What could I possibly say to reverse the damage of having to live with those memories?

"Why did you tell Dane about it?" I asked.

"Because he saw the scar, and at the time, it had been eating away at me. He just caught me at the right moment is all."

I pulled her to me, and buried my face in her nest, breathing in the musky scent of her womanly essence. What I mostly got was the aroma of freshly bathed skin, which turned me on just as much. Shannon tried to pull her panties back up, but I was just persistent enough, and she gave up, easily. After we'd made love, she asked me how I could love a marked girl like her.

"You're not marked," I assured her. "It was just some fucked up game your parents were playing. Sick, yes... paranormal, I don't think so."

She spent the night with me, and she seemed comforted, to rest in my arms. In the morning, after she'd left, I began to think about what she'd said. With this information, a lot of things began to make sense, like why Shannon had really gotten mad at Dane for asking her to shave, and why she got mad at me for asking her to tell me about it.

But even more, I began to understand her mood swings and inwardness, and then her compulsive sexual promiscuousness.

Her parents might not have turned her into an evil mistress, but they had done some definite damage to her soul.

I'll admit the possibility may exist that in the process of their debauched behavior, Aaron and Lindy could have inadvertently jeopardized their daughter's well being to the point of a partial possession by some kind of dark force, but as far as I could tell, as bad as the abuse was, the rest of it had been nothing more than sexual role playing that had gone horribly wrong.

.　.　.　.　.

The summer was beginning to wind down, and so were our gigs at the Canteen. For the final show we decided to surprise the audience, and the owner by going electric during our last set. Dane and I played two acoustic sets, and then we brought the Cooder brothers up on stage, to rock out the last eight songs. We introduced ourselves as The Moonlighters, and the crowd loved it. It was a fun gig, and it was one that I'll never forget.

It was around this time that Dane joined a country band called Hillbilly Deluxe, which featured a hot female singer named Jennifer Huxley. Not only is she good looking, but the girl knows how to work a crowd, and she can really sing.

Dane became their lead guitarist, playing with an array of instruments that included banjo, fiddle, and mandolin. He also added some fine lead and harmony vocals to their sound. Other players were Keith Andrews on rhythm guitar, Robbie King on bass, and Jeramiah Wheatly on drums.

We started doing shows in which Dane and I would open up for them, and then he would join them as the main act. After a while, most venues would only be willing to book Hillybilly Deluxe, so that was when I officially became their roadie. This was also the period in which Shannon had stopped coming to our shows, because first, Stephanie and Bethany were always there, and second, because Dane had started to have eyes for Jennifer's friend, Kathleen "Kat" Nicholson.

23

It was about noontime, when I was sitting on the front steps of my apartment building, checking out a camera that I'd just bought. I heard female voices down in front of the store, and I noticed Shannon's younger sister, Molly, talking to a friend who was getting into her car. Molly is a spitting image of her older sister, and every bit as hot, maybe even hotter, and she knows it. She's a little tease, and a little smart ass, as well.

After a minute or two had passed, the friend drove away, and Molly came up the sidewalk towards me. She sat down next to me, and after a few moments, she began to fidget.

"What's the matter, Molly?" I inquired.

She sighed, "Joshua…"

I said, "What is it, Molly?"

"I need to confess something," she replied.

"Okay… Go for it."

"Well… sometimes when I'm in class, and I look at Mr. Abernathy, my English teacher… I start to feel… funny."

Now she had my attention, and also Sluggo's attention, who upon hearing her last remark, had begun to perk up, and get in on the conversation, because both Sluggo and myself had become quite certain that this girl was catting for a fuck.

So, of course, I asked her in all sincerity to, "Please, go on."

"Well, when I go to the girl's room between classes, my underwear is all wet."

"Really?"

"Really," she said, "all... wet."

I said, "Come with me, Molly."

We went up to my place, and I asked her if she'd mind posing for a few photographs. She said that she would do it. I began to snap shot after shot, and I instructed her to begin to remove her clothes as we went. By the time she had discarded her panties, I had become so inebriated with desire for her that I could barely continue to operate the camera.

"Hey... Why am I the only one in the altogether here?" she protested. "I think the photographer should take his clothes off, too."

"It's only fair," I said in total agreement, and I wasted no time in reducing myself to her level of nakedness.

When I had lowered my pants, and Sluggo had sprung full mast from his man cave, Molly's eyes almost popped out of their sockets. The thought suddenly occurred to me that she could possibly still be a virgin. The idea did not deter me. I asked her to lie on the bed, and spread her legs.

"I want you to think about Mr. Abernathy, Molly. Don't touch yourself. Only think about him."

At first, she became flush with embarrassment, but I continued to gently prod her, and after awhile, I noticed that her vulva had begun to glisten. A few moments later, her honey had begun to run out of her like a river. It was all that I could take.

I crawled between her legs, and began to lap her juicy fig, and then I said, "This isn't your first time... is it, Molly?"

She said, "No silly. My first was Mr. Abernathy."

I'd taken a moment to ponder this revelation, when most inconveniently, there was a knock at my door.

"Who the fuck is this?" I wondered out loud.

And then Molly said, "Oh, that's Shannon. I called her, and told her I'd be here, so she could pick me up."

"Great," I replied.

How much more inconvenient could it get?

I let Shannon in, and right off the bat, she started yelling at me.

"What the fuck are you doing with my sister!?"

"Oh… you know…" I stuttered.

I'd found myself at a loss for words, and unlike a few moments before, I was tongue-tied. Then I got the bright idea to explain to her that I'd been putting together a book of photographs, and that Molly had agreed to be one of my subjects. I had thought it was a good sell, but Shannon wasn't buying it.

"You're making a book!? Oh wow, that sounds awesome! And how do you do it, with your face in my sister's twat? Ohh… I get it… It's a close up, right?"

Apparently, she had gotten a bird's eye view from the front window. I really hate that window.

She continued, "Can I be in it, too? Is my picture gonna be in it?"

"I was considering it," I answered truthfully.

"Well, I don't want it in there!"

Molly said, "Oooh, can I be in it? Can I, can I!?"

"No, you can't!" Shannon scolded.

"Awww, but I wanna!"

Shannon gave Molly the kind of look that said, *Shut up or die*, and Molly got the message.

Then, to my surprise, she said, "Okay, Joshua… let's take some pictures."

I decided to run with it, so I told Molly to just simply pose in any manner that she'd like. I began to snap a sequence of unbelievably erotic pics, as Molly naturally breezed through every tantalizing position that she could think of. Finally, after she'd given her all, she plopped down onto the bed feigning exhaustion.

The next thing I knew, Shannon had crawled between Molly's legs, and had buried her tongue into her sex. As astonishing as this had seemed to me, I'd still had enough presence of mind to realize my good fortune, so I continued to snap a few more pics, but when Molly began to come, I lost control, and I had to put the camera down, because I just couldn't figure out how to take pictures, and masturbate at the same time.

At this point, I would have made the connection with Shannon, but she still had her clothes on. I climbed behind her, anyway, and I began to feel her up, and then I tried to unbutton her blouse. That's when she shoved me off of her, and got up from the bed.

She motioned for me to take her place between Molly's legs, and when I hesitated, she ordered me to, "Do it!"

Molly's bush was as soft as the hair on a baby's head, and I can't remember tasting a sweeter pussy, ever. I wanted her bad, but I was trying half heartedly to restrain myself from having her. Shannon took care of that dilemma when she told Molly to fuck me.

Molly got on her hands and knees, and in that sexy little nymphet voice of hers, she said, "Spank me first."

I said, "What?"

"Spank me... make it sting."

I looked at Shannon, and she said, "Go ahead, spank the little witch."

I returned my attention to Molly, and as I gazed upon that tight, nubile bottom, I swear, my dick stretched another inch in length.

Shannon persisted, "C'mon Joshua... Hit her!"

I raised my hand, and then I gave her what had amounted to nothing more than a love tap. Molly squealed in mock pain.

"Oooh, thank you, sir... Can I have another?"

I couldn't believe this. I had a horny, sixteen-year-old girl in my bed, who was a masochist, and obviously, so was Shannon. I was beginning to believe that maybe I really hadn't known her that well, after all. Judging by her actions, I was beginning to believe she was a sadist, as well.

But it did make sense, after what she had told me, and even though Molly was of the legal age of consent, I'd begun to feel as though I had been molesting her, too. Even so, once I saw her honey begin to flow out of her, and run down her thigh, I forgot all about that.

"Harder!" Shannon ordered.

This time, I put a little more smack into it, and within seconds, I could see my hand print beginning to appear on her ass. Molly began to rub herself between her thighs, and then she stared to moan.

"Look at her… the dirty little slut… hit her!" Shannon was now becoming visibly turned on. She had opened her pants, and had slid her hand down inside. The sight of her masturbating had made me grab my cock, and when Shannon had realized that I had begun to stroke myself, she began to rub herself even harder.

I guess Molly had begun to feel all alone, because she reminded me that I was supposed to be paying a little more attention to her tush. I don't know what had come over me, but I was becoming so turned on by all of this, that I began to spank her, hard, until she collapsed, prone onto the bed, and began to cry.

Her tender behind had really begun to redden, and just as I was about to feel sorry for her, Shannon had removed her belt, and said, "Here… use this."

It was as though Shannon's voice had begun to sap me of my will. I took the belt from her, and without any hesitation, I began to whip Molly, until her entire rear end had started to turn black and blue.

"Stop," she begged.

Shannon had fingered herself to orgasm during Molly's beating, and now, she ordered me to fuck her. I pulled Molly up from the bed and pushed myself into her in one slow thrust, I watched her vulva begin to spread and envelope me, until my entire length had disappeared inside of her. She moaned her appreciation, and I continued to observe our coupling, as I slid my honey soaked cock in and out of her.

It wasn't long before I had begun to feel that familiar rumble deep in my lions, and Molly must have felt it, too, because she bounced me off of her, and said, "Me, on top."

Again, I watched her tight little pussy wrap itself around my pole, and again, I watched myself disappear inside of her. She began to fuck me, her sweet black and blue behind smacking my thighs, and now there was no way that I was gonna be able to stop myself from coming. She knew this, and she moaned for me to hang on.

"Just a little more," she whimpered. "Just a little..."

And then, she was coming, and then I was coming, and I filled her with so much semen, that I'd swear that it almost pushed her off of me.

She patted my chest and said, "Now, fuck Shannon."

Then she rolled off of me, and Shannon, who was now out of her clothes, climbed on top of me. Molly lay there, right next to us, and watched us fuck, her fingers inserted firmly into her sex. Shannon gazed at her for a second, and then she slowly began to glide up and down on me, keeping rhythm with Molly, who had begun to plunge her fingers in and out of herself, as if in a trance.

Shannon looked down at me, and said, "I'm starting to think that you and Dane really are brothers."

"And why is that?" I asked.

"Cause you both seem to like to spread the mayonnaise on a nice sister sandwich."

"Hey... What Dane does on his own time is his business... But I gotta hand it to ya... I do like your mayo analogy."

"Yeah... put the mayo on the bun."

"Hey... you're good."

"I know... I... Uhhh... Mmmm..."

Afterwards, as the three of us lay side by side, I said, "So... this is all about revenge?"

Shannon jumped up and said, "What the fuck is that supposed to mean?"

"It means, that you pay Dane back for screwing the Swanson sisters, by arranging a sex romp with his best friend and a couple of Morrison sisters. You fucked up, you should've had Rowen here, too… Then you could've triple sized him."

"You fucking jerk! You so don't know what you're talking about! You have to fuck everything that moves! Aren't I good enough!? I might have done this because I wanted to treat you to something good. Maybe, I just wanted to be with you! But since you had to say that stupid shit… You can forget it!"

"Ohh, would you two… just… shut… up!"

Molly was back on top of me. She had somehow managed to climb over Shannon, sit on me, and grind her wet muff into me, until I had begun to stiffen up, again.

After she'd accomplished her mission, and had contently begun to ride me like a pony at the county fair, she continued, "And what a boring bunch of shit. Can't a girl just get fucked? Why don't you just go fuck your own boyfriend, Shannon. You're really fucking weird."

24

In just a couple of months, Hillbilly Deluxe had taken off, and had gained a huge following. Between Jennifer's authentic country twang, and Dane's fancy country picking, it was easy to figure out why. They'd already reached the point where they'd found themselves booked solid, every Thursday through Saturday night, for months.

They'd put some money together, and had T-shirts made, which they sold at their shows. Everybody was wearing them. Dane had begun the practice of recording their shows, and they were also in the process of recording a demo of original compositions, and a few choice cover songs.

It had always been Jennifer's dream to go to Nashville. It just so happened that she had been a good friend of another established country singer, who'd invited the Hillbillies to join him in Nashville, as his opening act for a few gigs in December. By the time they'd returned from the first trip, they had decided that they would all move there for while, and try to hit the big time.

For Dane, it was a no brainer. Despite Jennifer's solid vocal ability, it was he who'd possessed the real talent. Jennifer would even admit it, night after night, when she'd explain to the audience that even though the band had been together for some time before, it had been Dane who'd been the missing ingredient that they needed to really click.

Not only had Dane been the one to complete their sound, but it had been easy to see that he had also begun to assert himself as the leader of the band, which didn't sit real well with Jennifer. The other members of the band loved it, because now they had someone who could lead them through the sweeping instrumental breaks and tempo changes that every true musician lives for.

With each show, I watched them grow tighter and tighter, and I'd never seen Dane enjoy himself on stage as much as he had, during this period. I told him so, and I also reminded him that not only would he have a great time playing in Nashville, but that he was also a great recording engineer, and that he'd have no trouble finding work in one of the studios on Music Row. He already knew it.

The only other question had been whether Shannon would accompany Dane to Nashville, or not. Dane had become interested in Jennifer's friend, Kat, and had openly begun to pursue her affection. They had finally hooked up during the first trip to Nashville, but Kat is a good person, and she could see that Shannon loved Dane, so she had purposely let things cool between them, even though she'd truly begun to have feelings for him.

Of course, Dane could never completely isolate himself into one genre of music. He and I continued to play a show here and there, and once Hillbilly Deluxe had committed to Nashville, they could no longer book as many shows locally, so he and I began to attend a few Friday night jam sessions at Tubby's Barn, as well.

During the time of our absence, a whole bunch of new players had begun to join in on the sessions. Brent and the Cooder brothers were still there. Sam was still pounding the skins, but now, Brent had moved to drums, as well, as part of a two-drummer set up. Philo had moved from bass to keyboards, and an old regular named Sherwood Mason had taken over the bass duties.

A very interesting guitar player named Eric Cummings had joined up, and had kind of taken over Dane's old position as session leader. This guy was all over the place, but in a good way. You could easily hear in his playing that not only had he been influenced by the usual rock and roll jam bands, but he'd also been well versed in jazz, flamenco, and blues, as well.

When Sherwood took a break, and Dane had stepped in on bass, Eric immediately picked up on his superior abilities, and the fact that he could follow his exotic tempo changes on a dime. He began to push Dane, and the rest of the guys into musical progressions that were absolutely out of sight.

The icing on the cake was Alan Fricke, a singer and lyricist, who played a Hammond B3 organ, and who also possessed the voice of an old black blues guy. He had been co-writing and recording a demo with Dane over the past several months, but the work had been sporadic, because they had both been swamped with other commitments.

In any event, anyone who had been there during any of those nights, could not deny that they had been treated to some of the finest and most interesting progressive music ever made, and once again, I had been impressed by something that I'd always known first hand, which was how easily Dane could slide in with anybody, and play any type of music, both fluently and daringly. You could easily see that while Eric had compelled Dane to reach past those uncharted musical boundaries, Dane had inspired Eric to do the same.

．　．　．　．　．

During Christmas, Dane and I had decided to take a trip to Gettysburg. The lease on his house was soon to expire, so we figured that we'd use it one more time. We visited Val, and Clayton, and of course, we just could not resist hooking up with Gabrielle and Dawn Marie, who had both been very happy to see us.

Shannon had still been a little put off with me for my comments during our tryst with Molly, back in September. Now, since our weekend in Gettysburg, she was mad at Dane, because she had been sure that he'd spent time with Gabrielle.

Despite herself, she called me, and asked me why Dane had stopped inviting her to come to his shows. I knew that it was because he'd still been smitten with Kat, but I had told her that it had probably been because she had led him to believe that she was no longer interested.

"Dane told me that you dissed one of the songs that he wrote with Jennifer," I explained. "He said that you told him the song was stupid."

"I never said that!" she assured me.

I said, "Well, why don't you just call him, and say that you want to go to a show with him?"

Then, I told her that I was almost positive that neither Bethany nor Stephanie would be at the show that Friday night, at a place called The Shady Rest.

Shannon took my advice, and Dane took her to the show, but she sulked the entire time, and she wouldn't talk to anybody. Kat had left early, and there was no Stephanie and Bethany, so I figured that she was just pissed off at Dane, for looking a little too cozy with Jennifer, on stage.

It was true that the two of them had developed a strong visual chemistry through their performances that had become part of the band's appeal. Shannon just couldn't deal with it. What she didn't realize was that she'd never had any cause to worry in the first place, because Jennifer prefers the company of women.

It had been planned the week before that Dane and I would do a set to open the show, but Jennifer had been suffering with a cold all week long, and she knew that her voice wouldn't last the night. So, we decided to play it by ear, so to speak, and as it turned out, we would up helping to close out the show.

Towards the end of our set, Dane and I played one of our usual songs called, "Glace Bay Blues," which we had invited Keith to come up and join in on. The song itself works as a kind of jazz blues fusion, and it features me on harmonica, but in the second of two instrumental breaks, Dane and I trade off leads. It's kind of a drowsy number, from which we then segue into a standard blues riff.

Dane signaled for Robbie and Jeremiah to come up, and as we shifted gears, they began to provide us with some bottom. This of course, was another song that featured my harmonica, and plenty of room for Dane's guitar. We took our time before Dane began to sing the first of the song's three verses.

The Hillbillies had built up a pretty loyal following at The Shady Rest, and a lot of the same people had been showing up, week after week. I knew that this would be their last show there, before they went to Nashville. So, I wanted to give both the band and the audience a kind of personal send off that they could share together, and always remember.

I had written the lyrics for the song that afternoon, and when I showed them to the guys, right before the show, they were delighted, because the song mentioned The Shady Rest, and motorcycles, and "women wearin' nothin' but my cowboy hat." I titled it, "Shady Rest Blues," which just tickled the owners, and the audience to pieces.

We jammed it out for about fifteen minutes, Dane and I trading solos back and forth, between verses.

Towards the end, I yelled, "Let me sing the blues for y'all!" and I repeated the last verse.

Dane just smiled at me. We finished the song, and the crowd went bananas.

Dane yelled, "We call that one, "Shady Rest Blues"!"

They went even crazier.

Then Dane said, "I don't know who this guy is!" referring to me. "I found him on the side of the road!"

I said, "Yeah… I've got a bad habit of wandering through cornfields, and coming out lost on the other side!"

The whole place erupted with laughter, and then Dane said, "No… that's my brother… I think I'll keep him."

A collective, "Aaahhhh," then resounded from the female part of the crowd.

Little did they know, that the comical and heartfelt exchange had been a part of every show that Dane and I had ever done.

As I was leaving the stage, I saw Dane talking to Keith, and then he grabbed me, and said, "One more."

He called Jennifer up to the stage, and the whole band did a song called "Can't You See."

Dane played the intro, on guitar and harmonica, and then I started in on the verse. For the chorus, Dane and Jennifer sang the harmonies, and Dane played solos in between.

We stretched it out for ten minutes, and Dane was fired up, and when Dane gets fired up, I get fired up. Then, the rest of the band got fired up. We sang and played our asses off, and as Dane says, it was badass. So then, the audience got fired up, too. Just as I was about to sing the line in the last verse, "Take me a southbound, all the way to Georgia," Dane leaned into me, and said into my ear, "Nashville."

So, I sang "Nashville" instead of "Georgia" and the crowd went nuts, because Jennifer had told them earlier that the Hillbillies were going to play there, for keeps. I looked over at Jennifer, and she was smiling from ear to ear. The place was rockin', and on Dane's cue, we slammed through a couple more choruses, and then it was over.

I hugged Dane, and told him that it had been great, and that I loved him. I had to hide my tears, because I knew that this might have been the last time that I would play with him, for awhile.

There is nothing like playing in front of a live audience. As a musician, you feed off them, and if it's good, you become one with them, and it's magic. I love it, and the best part about it, is that I got to do it with Dane. I'll cherish it, forever. But Dane was doing great, and it was time for him to move on to bigger and better things.

I made my way to the bar, and the Hillbillies played an encore of a couple songs, finishing with "Brown Eyed Girl," which had the whole place dancing and singing along. As I walked by Shannon, I could see that she was thoroughly pissed off, and consumed with jealousy that everyone else had been having a good time, except her. She just could not see that it was her own fault.

As we were packing up, she went out to the van, and quietly sat in the front seat, waiting to leave. I walked around to her side, and tapped on her window to talk to her, but she just stared straight ahead, and she wouldn't look at me.

I said, "C'mon, Shannon… Roll down the window," but she ignored me.

When I moved back over to where Dane and the others had been loading their vehicles, Keith asked me, "What's wrong with Shannon?"

I said, "I don't know… she's weird."

He said, "I know."

Dane had been standing there the whole time, listening to us. What could he say? Shannon had embarrassed him in front of every friend that he'd ever had.

. . . . .

It was still up in the air, as to whether Shannon had planned to go with Dane to Nashville, but in any case, she had decided to throw him a going away party. The idea being, to show everyone that she'd supported his decision, and that the two of them were solid. She stayed close by his side the entire evening, as if she'd finally realized that it had been in her best interest to once again, fully commit herself to protecting her investment.

But the huggie and kissie routine had pissed, at least, a couple people off. Even I had believed it to be a ruse. The way she'd made a point of gabbing with me had made me feel as though she'd simply needed me in the act, as well. I figured that it had all been a thinly veiled attempt to show Stephanie and Bethany, and anyone else who'd been interested, that in the end, Dane would always prefer to be with her.

Whatever Shannon's point had been, Stephanie was still there to assure her that she was not just going to sit still, and and let everything be peachy.

While Bethany quietly ignored Shannon, Stephanie had implied several times that, "I hate that little slut!"

And, of course, she'd made sure that she'd said it loud enough, so that Shannon could hear it.

She asked me, "How can you stand to put your dick into that dirty little cunt?!"

It had become clear that Stephanie was looking for a fight. Even Bethany had begun to sit there, nervously pretending that none of this had been happening.

At one point, Erin, who by now had obviously begun to regret the fact that she had been the one who had invited these girls to the party, turned and looked at Stephanie, and said, "Really…!? They're sitting right there!"

I tried to avoid her, but she had done a swell job of getting herself really liquored up, and pissed off, and she found me, and then she tore into me like a woman who had just realized that she had begun to menstruate into the crotch of her favorite panties. She went on and on, and after a while, I just began to get the idea that we were no longer just talking about Dane and Shannon.

I told her that I didn't have an answer for her.

I said, "Maybe Bethany just got her wires crossed, about Dane."

"Oh, that's bullshit!" she snarled. "You men are all alike… You just use women!"

Gee, where have I heard those words, before?

25

I'm once again, sitting in the living room of my hot box of an apartment, suffering through another day of this cursed heat wave.

For a week, now, I've been sweating bullets, and I'm waiting for the 11 o'clock news report to tell me that, "Tonight, the National Academy of Planetary Sciences has confirmed, that the Earth has broken from its axis, and is now being pulled directly into the sun. Scientists have not provided an exact time frame, but meteorologist and amateur planetary researcher, none other than our own Herbert Snittleman, here at the Channel 11 News, has estimated that, within two to three weeks, the entire surface of the planet will be reduced to charcoal."

Because of these sweltering evenings, I've been operating on no sleep, and because I've been getting no sleep, I've begun to experience an acute decline in my capacity to think straight. Thus, I'm starting to believe that Herbert Snittleman's guesstimation may very well be possible.

The good news is that in light of the fact that I suspect we're all about to fry, I am no longer afraid to use my ceiling fan. Damn those fucking reaper barons down at the power plant, and besides, I'd rather bleed out from slashes and gashes, than be burned to a crisp till I'm cinders and ashes. Hey, I'll bet that even Otis would like that one.

Speaking of Otis, he is no longer with us. No, he's not dead, at least I don't think so. They finally did kick him out, though, and he'd made a pretty big scene over it, with the usual ranting and raving. As usual, he had already been well on his way to filling up his tank, when he had made his way down to the Hotel to top himself off.

Stormy told me that eventually, Otis had begun to insult everyone in the place, when Big Red kind of took it personal, and had physically thrown him out on to the street, where he staggered into traffic, causing a three car collision, in which one vehicle had plowed over a fire plug, effectively turning the town square into a water fountain.

The strange part is that during the entire melee, Otis had vanished, and no one had seen him, since, although there have been rumors that he wound up in Wild Wood, New Jersey, where he'd drunkenly pulled the lever on a slot machine, and had won a couple hundred grand. In any event, authorities are still interested in his whereabouts, because he remains their number one suspect in the capital offense of causing a catas-trophe.

Anyway, even with all of the excitement, I did manage to finish that letter to Sara, and send it off to her, but she won't be there to receive it, simply because she is back in town, and so is Agnes. I received a call from Sara, yesterday, inviting me to join the two of them for a beer, down at the Hotel.

Apparently, Sara had caught her husband, and his secretary doing the horizontal bop on top of the desk in his office, after business hours. She'd left him and took him to the cleaners in the process. In the meantime, Agnes had moved out there, and she has been sharing a bed with Sara in Tempe, Arizona for almost a year and a half, now, not counting the amount of time that she had spent coming back here to wreak havoc on several relationships, which had all been part of a fiendish plan that had been hatched by Sara.

I guess she'd requested my letter, as a means of finding out if her plan had worked. When I hadn't immediately responded, she had simply lost patience, and then decided that she and Agnes would return here together to take care of any loose ends. I had been sorry to inform her that she'd arrived about a day too late, because Dane and Shannon had left for Nashville, only the day, before.

I had been sorry to give Sara the news, but not for her. A couple of days before they'd left, Shannon had invited me to take a walk with her out to one of her favorite places on the Bruckner property. She told me that she had made up her mind to go to Nashville with Dane.

I had tried my best, as we walked, to encourage her that everything would be great for the two of them. Then, like an idiot, I told her that I would always love her, and that if she'd ever change her mind, that I would dump whoever I might be with, to be with her.

In the gentlest way that she could, Shannon assured me that she planned on marrying Dane, and having kids with him.

I said that I understood, and then I asked her, "Can ya blame me?"

She just smiled that half smile of hers that she couldn't hide, even when she'd been trying to be serious, and said, "I can blame you for a lot of things, Joshua."

We continued walking, until we'd reached the creek that winds its way through the property. As we stood there skipping stones across the water, a light sprinkle had begun to filter down through the trees.

I suggested that we head back, before the impending deluge had arrived, but Shannon laughed and said, "Let's get wet."

The thought of getting caught in the rain with her had definitely seemed like a pleasurable experience, and I let those feelings overcome me. Within moments, the heavens had opened up on us, and it wasn't long before the both of us were drenched, and laughing at our supposed misfortune.

As the rain continued to pelt us, I took the time to really see Shannon, and I thought how beautiful she had looked with the rain cascading down her face, water dripping from her chin. Our laughter soon evolved into a loving gaze, as our eyes locked.

Almost instinctively, we embraced. The feeling of our clothed, but wet bodies pressing together, sent waves of arousal through me, and like that first time that she had come to me, I knew that she had sensed me longing for her.

The sensation of her wet lips pressed into mine, had sent the feeling from my head, directly to its intended destination, and as I'd hardened, even more, Shannon pressed herself against me, her own body yearning for what, but for a thin layer of clothing, she would soon have deep inside of her.

I can't even begin to describe how it had felt to make love to her, naked in the rain, that day. I had realized that it might have been the last time that I would ever make love to her, again, and it was then I knew for sure that I had never, and would never, love anyone the way that I loved her.

Shannon's departure had left an emptiness inside of me, that had only just begun to put me down for the count, when Bethany had decided to pay me a visit. She told me that Stephanie was pregnant, and that she was sure that the kid was mine. Again, a girl had gotten herself knocked up, and she was claiming that I had been responsible.

"Fuck! Doesn't any woman in this town use contraceptives!?"

I had begun to suspect conspiracy in the making, but Bethany assured me that Stephanie had been in love with me for a long time, and that she would be willing to have an abortion if I didn't want the kid. I am not in love with Stephanie, but I don't necessarily find the idea of living with her to be all that bad.

She's a beautiful girl. Guys line up to ask her out. She can be a witch, but I admit that I have a lot more in common with her than most girls I've been attracted to, and I won't let her get an abortion. She and I need to talk.

Suddenly, it has begun to seem as though my whole world is crashing in around me. The common traits between my father and myself have become too many to simply deny, and I'm not proud of it. The past week has been so depressing, that at one point, I had seriously begun to contemplate suicide. But last night, just as I was about to loosen the bolts on my ceiling fan, an angel knocked at my door.

It had taken Gina less than five minutes to tell me why she'd left New York. Apparently, it had been the last straw, when she came home to find her mother, in the process of attempting to have sex in every position depicted in the *Kama Sutra*, with a self-proclaimed Buddhist monk, on the living room floor. When I told her that she had come to the wrong place, because I had seriously been thinking about converting to Buddhism, she did not laugh.

As we were getting ready for bed, I noticed that she had been wearing the very same pair of jeans, with the persnickety fly that she had worn the first time that we'd ever fooled around. I told her honestly that she looked more beautiful than ever, and then I made the comment that her jeans had looked as though they had been made just to fit her perfect rear end.

"Why sweetheart, you're so kind. What could it possibly be that you're buttering me up for?" she laughed.

"Only to get into those jeans."

"Oh, right… these jeans. Well, I seem to remember, now that I swore never to let you into them, again."

I chuckled, "It's obvious that you weren't able to keep that promise."

Gina considered my argument for a second, and then she smiled. She stripped down to her panties, climbed onto the bed, and opened her legs.

"In that case, I'm going to wet these for you."

She began to move her fingers in a circular motion against her crotch. Instinctively, I grabbed hold of my dick, and began to stroke myself.

"Careful, babe," she scolded. "I want you in me, when you come."

She pulled her panties aside, and slid a finger into her opening. I almost lost it right then, and when she grazed her fingers down her thigh, she purposely left a trail of honey for me to see. This was all that I could take. I crawled between her legs, and pushed my tongue inside of her.

Gina closed her eyes, and let herself enjoy the moment, but it wasn't long before the attention that I'd been giving her had begun to make her body undulate with anticipation, and soon, she was on the verge.

Almost frantically, she quivered, "Inside, Joshua... You're gonna make me..." and then, she pulled me to her, and guided me into her aching wound.

The sensation of having her crotch filled with my throbbing penis had sent her over the edge.

She squeezed me, tight, her voice breathless, "Now, Joshua... Come now!"

The sight of this beautiful girl, letting herself lose complete control of her body had pushed me past the point of no return, as well. Her wish was my command.

As we drifted off to sleep, I told her that I had meant what I'd said.

"It's the truth... about you bein' beautiful and all."

She asked me, "Joshua... Am I normal, now? Are we normal?"

I took a moment to ponder the question, and I began to wonder just what normal had been. On top of everything else that had happened, recently, both Ranae, and Brigid had begun to visit me, pretty regularly, in my house. As a matter of fact, I had taken a shower with Ranae, only a few days before, and about a week ago, I'd had a dream that Brigid had shot me, the bullet lodging in my spine, paralyzing me. Then, she lay prone on top of me, put the gun to her head, and blew her brains out.

This kind of stuff begs me to ask of myself, the same question I'd asked about my Dad. Do I indeed possess the capability to interact with the dead, or is it the simple possibility that I happen to be going insane?

"Joshua... Joshua... Are you awake? You can't have fallen asleep, already."

"Ya, I'm here… Yes, we're good. But let's not get completely normal. Where would be the fun in that?"

She snuggled tight against me, "I know, right?"

Anyway, let me swing this all back around to the present, and my fascination with the significance of interplanetary sunburn. Earlier this evening, after Gina had gone out with Heather, somewhere, I had received a phone call from Dane.

"Well, c'mon Bro… aren't you gonna congratulate me?!"

"Alright… I congratulate you… but why?"

"Cause I'm gonna be a daddy!" he drawled.

"Wow… Yes… Congratulations. Dude, I'm happy for ya."

My mind suddenly began to race. I started to picture Shannon in the birthing room at the hospital, crying and smiling, as the doctor presented me with my first look at our baby boy.

"Hey, you still there Bro?" Dane's voice had snapped me out of it.

"Hey, do me a favor, Bro, and give Shannon my regards."

"Right, Bro… She's in the shower, now, but I sure will."

After the conversation had ended, I began to picture Shannon, wet in the shower, just like she'd been in the woods, only a few days, before.

Her words, "and having kids with him," had begun to possess my thoughts.

I started to think about Gina's mother, and her sudden prurient interest in Hindu mythology, which has prompted me to consider the Buddhist belief that suffering is caused by desire, and that the way to end suffering is through an enlightenment that enables one to halt an endless sequence of births and deaths to which one is, otherwise subjected to.

On the other hand, some people who believe in hell, insist that it's a place where you must endlessly suffer to the point of madness, from having to deal with something that had caused you torment in life, over and over, again.

So, as I sit here, waiting for Herbert Snittleman to warn me of my impending demise, I can't help but wonder if I should simply make a resolution to give up all desire for earthly pleasure, especially the pleasures of the flesh? Or am I already dead, and if I am, does the possibility exist that I'm doomed to relive the torment of my mistakes for eternity?

Well, as Dane would say, "Does Pinocchio have wooden balls?"

Also by Richard Henshaw:

Tangled In Blue

Available via lulu.com

www.ingramcontent.com/pod-product-compliance
Lightning Source LLC
Chambersburg PA
CBHW071200260626
47162CB00003B/1115